New Rotterdam Quartet

K. C. Bacon

New Rotterdam Quartet
Copyright 2021 by K.C. Bacon

All rights reserved. No portion of this book may be reproduced, stored in a retrieval system, or transmitted in any form or by any means—electronic, mechanical, photocopy, recording, scanning, or other—except for brief quotations in critical reviews or articles without the prior written permission of the author. To obtain permission, contact the editor:

editors@emerald-books.com

Bellus Books
USA

ISBN: 978-1-954779-30-3

CONTENTS

Birth Of The Cool	1
Halvard Sees The World	49
Hong's Moral	101
The Magical Smelt	152

IV

To My Brothers and Sisters

VI

Birth Of The Cool

For Rolf Olsen

Frank and I grew up in Devilbridge, the rotten part of New Rotterdam, a neighborhood notable for vacant storefronts, potholes, and unruly children like me and Frank. To get to Devilbridge, you travel north on Washcon Avenue for a few miles until you see The Pearly Gate Tavern. The Pearly Gate is famous for its sign above the bar: 'WELCOME TO DEVILBRIDGE - GOOD LUCK, YOU'LL NEED IT.

At the eastern foot of Hallowed Hill, Devilbridge's primary geographical hallmark, sits New Rotterdam's first cemetery. It holds the gravestones of many early New Rotterdam movers and shakers. All the dead Vander Hoeks are planted there, Devilbridge being the former site of Emil Vander Hoek's dairy and pasture lands. The land went up for sale after Vander Hoek's wife went mad and slaughtered all their cows, an event known in Greater

New Rotterdam lore as "Rotten Greta's Revenge." She is especially remembered at The Pearly Gate, where they serve the "Rotten Greta." One-third Aquavit, one-third apricot juice, one-third beet juice, and served with your choice of stirrer: beef jerky or celery stick. If you can drink two Rotten Gretas, a third one is free. Good Luck.

. . . .

Frank and I lived in Castle Moat, a housing development gone to seed. Every city has a neighborhood it wishes to forget. For New Rotterdam it is Devilbridge, and for me and Frank it was Castle Moat.

Kids from New Rotterdam called us Moaties. We called them Termites. Over time we developed a defensive technique called the Moatie Throatie. It was a hatchet chop to a Termite's neck. I've delivered just one Moatie Throatie in my lifetime. It was at the Wompburger after a football game between our Demons and the hated Wood Academy Woodies. My prey was a Woodie, a particularly virulent form of Termite. I delivered it through the Woodie's open window. But I hit a seat belt instead of his throat, breaking my finger. The Woodies howled with glee as I slunk away. I'm sure it was Frank that intervened on my behalf so that I wasn't made to walk home.

There were once five Lutheran Churches in Devilbridge, but by the time I was made to attend, there was one. Immanuel Lutheran Church. It's on N. 33rd, not far from the Wompbuger, and takes up an entire city block. Constructed of gray colored, biotite granite taken from the rocky bluffs beyond Satsapoo Nation, Immanuel Lutheran lost its roof in a fire a few years ago and its shell now languishes, waiting to be redeemed. When Frank and I were in school, Immanuel had a full congregation and my mother insisted I attend each Sunday, saying, "If it's good enough for God, it's good enough for you."

My mother seldom listened to her own advice. She was a part-time member at best. In fact, she'd only attend if there was a cake and pie sale going on. She said she was after recipes first, God second.

My mother was a good and kind woman who didn't like to be wrong. Going to Immanuel Lutheran in order to filch recipes wasn't wrong in her book. Rather, it was just another proof of the existence of God. She laughed, "He maketh me work in wondrous ways." She was a weird one, my mom. Lovable and fun, smart and weird.

God is a big deal in Devilbridge. Devilbridgers don't go to church as they once did, but that doesn't mean they don't admire God. Sure, they'll curse The Maker all day long, nastiest stuff you've ever heard. But it's like cussing out your cousin. You can tell each other to go to hell for the entire year, but at Christmas dinner, there you are, passing Aunt Freida's baked yams to each other. In fact, if you had to pick between getting your ass royally kicked by a gang of Devilbridge Diablos because you cut one of them off in traffic, or standing in line at the South Washcon Food Bonanza next to a Devilbridge mom after having disrespected God, it wouldn't matter. Your odds suck either way.

. . . .

Castle Moat had neither a castle nor a moat, though it did have an ornate iron gate barely attached to two pillars of brick that constantly needed repair and never received it. The iron gate was buttressed by concrete pillars, referred to by its residents as "The Monument," and was originally intended to give the project a sheen of respectability. Competing neighborhoods were Moran Street's "Sylvan Hills," notable for its lack of trees, and North Pointer Estates, named after the most foreboding street in Devilbridge, noted for the variety of its human flaw. The most popular Christmas gift at North Pointer Estates was a padlock.

Like me and Frank, and unlike North Pointer Estates, Castle Moat had ambition, however fanciful. For instance, initial Castle Moat homeowners were given architectural options with their purchase. Discriminating buyers could choose a ranch style home with garage in back or a ranch style home with garage in front. A broken wagon wheel could be added to the front porch. One could also get a house with a carport, sans garage. Houses with carports came with a high entryway, so stylish buyers could opt for a chandelier, choosing between one that appeared to be made of silver broom handles, or a metal one with white lights that twinkled.

My house was wagon wheel with garage in front and Frank's had the garage in the back, no wagon wheel. Neither of us had chandeliers, though Arnie McCowber did. In the sixth grade, Arnie used his chandelier as a swing in order to break his arm. He was class hero for a month.

Our house was clean, compact and comfortable, a bit smaller than Frank's because his father had had transformed their garage into an extra bedroom before Frank was born. They were a family of eight, whereas we were a family four. Me, mom and dad, and sister Shirley who eventually eloped to Florida with a guy who worked in a circus. After she realized she made a mistake, Shirley moved back to Devilbridge where she became a real estate appraiser, Pez addict, and full-time increasingly odd person. Still, my sister. What can you do?

Frank had a huge extended family in addition to his own. They came and went, mostly in the summer months when Frank's mother put them up in backyard tents.

"How many at your house today, Frank?" someone would ask.

"Don't know, can't count that high," Frank would answer, affecting the voice of Mr. Tribbleton, our middle school PE teacher. How Frank could manipulate his Adam's apple to look like Tribbleton's, I'll never know. No doubt, Frank could have been a successful actor had he not chosen instead to make his way as a workers' compensation attorney, specializing in longshoremen with bad backs.

As for me, I became a minor poet and office manager dabbling in losing money in the stock market.

. . . .

According to Frank's father, everything bad was caused by Republicans, whereas my father felt Democrats were the scourge of the earth. Though their sons were the best of friends, each father thought the other a dunce. Still, they put up with each other because of me and Frank. Once, during Moat Days, the Castle Moat summer festival organized by whichever parent lost the ritual drawing of straws, Frank and I were paired with our fathers in a boiled egg eating contest. Both teams were disqualified after our fathers started throwing eggs at each other.

My father was a good guy, though a gloomy guy. He seemed always to be gnawing at some inner agony. He gave the impression of someone with an irritated soul. Every once in awhile, my mother would smile big and get in his face. "Come on, where's the fun guy I married?" she'd say, inches from his nose. He'd invariably kiss her sweetly, after she jabbed her finger into his belly. That's when he was happiest, when my mother proved to him that she thought he was worth saving. He knew he wasn't much of a prize, but as long as his wife didn't catch on, he was safe.

Take it like a man was my father's philosophy. Be prepared to suffer. Life wins in the end, not you. It does it by lurking around every corner, waiting to snuff you out, so you better keep your wits about you. He learned his philosophy from my grandfather, who said the object of the game of life is to hold on for as long as you can, no matter how bad it gets. My father's side of the family weren't a lot of fun, and I avoided them as much as I could.

My father was a committed grunter. The noise was long, without nuance, a growling simper. I am grateful to have inherited my father's brown eyes, his intelligent forehead and length of leg, and even more grateful not to have inherited his grunt.

Happily, my mother doted on me. I was her guy, and I gravitated to her rather than to my dad. She was simply more fun to be with. Frank gravitated to my mother, too, his mother being a major sourpuss and his father the one who caused it. Like my father, Frank's dad worked the New Rotterdam docks as a longshoreman. Unlike my father, Frank's worked nights. That allowed him to spend daylight hours on his favorite stool at The Pearly Gate.

Castle Moat houses were close together, barely enough room for the dogs. As it happened, no Castle Moat family had less than one dog and most had more. Mine was named Squirrel and Frank's was Harp. The record for most dogs went to the Scallions on Mauve Circle. They had four Dachshunds, two Corgis, and a mentally unbalanced mutt named Ferguson. They also had seven kids. What can you say? Some people thrive on chaos and dog shit.

Mr. Scallion, incidentally, was much different than other dads. We never knew what he did for a living, but he always looked cool. He was like the neighborhood James Bond. A man of mystery. He favored faded Levis and tight t-shirts. I imagined him hanging out in Monte Carlo, frequenting the clubs, impressing the Euro trash. He'd waltz in, and inevitably someone from a far corner would gasp. It was easy to imagine Mr. Scallion leaning against the bar, looking around for danger. A good looker sidles up next to him and says, "Buy a girl a drink?"

"Depends," Mr. Scallion says, giving her the sly eye. "Do you thrive on chaos and dog shit?"

. . . .

As we entered high school, Frank and I thought of ourselves as smart kids. There were others. Jimmy Ballus, for instance. Face it, you have to be a pretty smart kid to climb into second story windows in order to rob ladies purses and not get caught until you're thirty-three. Jimmy, who was on the Demon tennis team with me, robbed houses all the time. He learned it from his uncle.

Once, our assistant tennis coach, Ms. Marnie, had her purse burgled. Jimmy felt so bad that he bought her and everyone else a round of sodas after practice. Jimmy paid with a crisp twenty dollar bill. Had anyone inspected it, they would have seen that Andrew

Jackson had grown a mustache with the help of Ms. Marnie's nephew's Sharpie.

During sophomore year, Frank and I invented names for people, beginning with ourselves. I was El Gelato and Frank, Master Sri. To us, most people were Eloi. Mr. Clocker, Devilbridge High's loquacious principal, was the chief Eloi. He was always lecturing everyone on topics they didn't care about. I never knew where Mr. Clocker lived, but he had an ex-wife and three kids who lived a few streets outside Castle Moat. He also dated Joan Flip's mom, Frannie. Frannie Flip had a mouth as big as Mr. Clocker's. People called her Fran the Nag. We called her the Eloi Queen.

In our early high school days, Frank and I trotted around Devilbridge like small town snobs, being philosophic about everything. No one was beneath our contempt, just as no fantasy was beyond our ken.

One day, Frank found me in the hallway in front of my locker.

"Being," he said.

"Being, yeah," I said. "That sounds deep." I believed, as Frank did, that by attaching the word "deep" to an observation instantly bestowed deepness on whatever nonsense you were spouting.

"Not too deep," Frank said, taking a breath.

"Yeah," I agreed. "Not too deep."

"No," Frank said. "We don't do too deep."

"Yeah," I said, drawing with my finger a circle in the air. "Too deep is like too round. Is is even possible to be too round?"

"Good analogy, man," Frank said, which was nice to hear as I thought I was only good at tennis and eating.

As we entered junior year, Frank and I often wasted time in the school library. Our school librarian, Mrs. Totter, was said to have once been a school principal, demoted for senility. She mostly slept in her chair like a barely breathing wax figure. Frank would sometimes sit next to her while she slept and mimic her soft snore while the rest of us snickered quietly. She was great fun asleep, and waking her was considered taboo.

One day, Frank found a book titled, "What Do You Want Out of Life?" He said it was about self-will and aspiration.

"I do not aspire to be an Eloi," I said.

Frank smiled. "Exactly," he said. "A worthy anti-aspiration." His eyes wandered into space. That was Frank's way when he was in deep thought. His eyes went goofy. Frank called it "seeing things as they really are." Frank was always a step ahead.

"Not many New Rotterdamers aspire, do they?" Frank asked rhetorically. His eyes went goofy again. Then he said, "New Rotterdam's population is what? 150,000?"

As it happened, I had only recently uncovered this fact for a report I was writing about a National Geographic article. Ms. Swish, our English teacher, said it was the only National Geographic article ever to mentioned New Rotterdam. While the article didn't mention Devilbridge, it did mention the Wood Academy twice because the author had gone to school there.

(On a side note, may I say that those prestigious twits over on Mt. Mary's Bluff can feel warm and fuzzy about themselves all they want, but the Scholars still lost to the Demons three times during my stint as chief smart ass of the tennis team. Here's a hint if you find yourself in a tennis match with a Wood Academy alum: They think trash talk is rude. Game over.)

"156,334 at last census," I said.

"Cool," said Frank. "So let's call it 150,000. The math is easier." Frank and I were both supporters of the Easy Math movement.

"From that amount," he continued, "we'll subtract pet lovers and Lutherans."

"Why pet lovers?"

"Because the only authentic aspirations of a pet lover is to kill you and save Fluffy."

"Reasonable," I said, believing pretty much anything Frank said was reasonable because it always was.

Frank stopped, bent slightly, breathing deeply. I thought he was going to throw up. Having ventured into thinking like a pet lover must have put him off. After several breaths, he continued.

"Naturally, being so messed up, pet lovers are wholly unable to manage higher thought, especially when it comes to philosophic matters like human aspiration."

"Reasonable."

Frank, anticipating my next question, said, "Of course, Lutherans can't be counted because they always think they know everything. And if you already know everything, the only aspiration you can possibly have is to become God. And I'm pretty sure God is Catholic, so good luck with that one."

"I agree with my mom," I said. "The only thing Lutherans get right are those pastries. Almond caramel cakes, cinnamon buns with vanilla custard."

"Rhubarb pie," Frank reminded me.

"Oh, God, yeah, rhubarb pie."

One of the enduring religious truths is that in the hands of Lutherans, rhubarb is rendered delectable by the inclusion of many cups of granulated sugar, thereby transforming it from vegetable to fruit. My mother told me that.

This reminds me of Mr. Poltice.

When any Castle Moat father said "You don't need to be a scientist to know that," he was quoting Mr. Poltice. Mr. Poltice was widely considered Devilbridge's most personable man. Lots of fathers tried to emulate him, none could. Mr. Poltice emceed every raffle at every Lutheran church in New Rotterdam for as long as anyone could remember, even though he was a lapsed Catholic with a Jewish wife. Perhaps Lutherans love rhubarb so much that it causes them to overlook minor heresies.

Mr. Poltice was the owner and grocer at Rottweiler Boys, a locally fancy grocery that held a huge annual Rhubarb Day sale. Two or three tents would be put up in the parking lot, manned by Lutheran ladies selling pies and pastries. $10 for a thin slice of Berthe's Famous Rhubarb Pie seemed like the deal of the century.

But Frank and I did not aspire to rhubarb pie. We had higher aspirations. We aspired to be cool.

For newly-minted sixteen year olds, being cool is the apex of human purpose.

. . . .

Ms. Swish, young and tall and extraordinarily blond, gave wicked glares to those who were tardy to her English class. It was her first year teaching at Devilbridge High, being a recent graduate of New Rotterdam University. Young enough to be our older sister, she looked like Wonder Woman. Shapely, athletic, gorgeous, her creamy blond hair fell like a waterfall down her graceful neck. Every girl was jealous of her and every boy fondled their pillows nightly, fantasizing they were kissing Ms. Swish.

We used to kid each other by suggesting connections with Ms. Swish. "Ms. Swish likes you." "Ms. Swish thinks you're cool." "You should marry Ms. Swish." Once, I received a book in the mail, *Being and Nothingness*. It had a Goodwill price tag on it. Inside the cover, next to the original dedication blacked out by a Sharpie, was written, "To My Very Favorite He-Man, Love, Ms. Swish." It was Frank's handwriting. I never read the book, though for years it performed admirably as a doorstop.

Ms. Swish was my first cool woman and, of course, you never forget your first. She was Frank's first cool woman, too. She used French words a lot, and since French words were cool, we spent a lot time practicing *joie de vivre* with *savoir faire*.

One way to determine if something is cool or not is to compare it with something obviously uncool. In this case, it was Mr. Freed, our disgusting history teacher.

I took several classes in high school from Mr. Freed, receiving an A each time only because I correctly guessed that Mr. Freed might be subject to flattery. Facing one of Mr. Freed's tests, I simply thought, "What kind of nonsense would make Freed feel good?"

Something was off about Mr. Freed. He was like a dud firework that fizzles after everyone has left. Prematurely bald and bunny-faced, I've never known anyone who chewed his mustache with as much gusto.

I saw Mr. Freed walking with Ms. Swish once. I thought I was going to puke. It was just after school began and Ms. Swish was still newly cool to me. I had been shadowing her when Mr. Freed entered the scene like a stray dog, instantly at her heel, panting. He was trying to speak with her and Ms. Swish was forced to half-turn and lean down to hear eager Mr. Freed, he being half a foot shorter. During one lean, their faces almost collided. Ms. Swish recoiled sharply with momentary distress. I wondered if she saw mustache hair between his teeth? That the two even spoke to each other was beyond contemplation, one being a Hollywood siren, the other a remnant of failed civilizations. One Yinalicious, the other just plain Yang.

Tres cool Ms. Swish was an admirer of Miles Davis, the coolest musician ever. Miles Davis's music was then enjoying a reprise, a revival. Cool, if it had ever been out, was back in. Ms. Swish's favorite tune of what she called "Miles's *oeuvre*" was from the 1958 recording, "The Birth of The Cool." The tune was the snappy, upbeat, foot-tapping "Jeru." While reading silently to ourselves, striving to comprehend Huck Finn, we'd often hear "Jeru" playing softly from her desk drawer. At the front of the class, behind her desk, sat cool Ms. Swish wearing sunglasses, bopping her head and drumming her fingers. Cool, Jeru. I didn't know who or what Jeru was, but I wished I were Jeru.

. . . .

We felt that being cool, as with any deep philosophy, must be based on firm intellectual principles, such as not ending up like Frank's cousin, Liam. Liam, ten years older than us, was rumored to be a really good ballplayer once, but to me he was a fat lump who spit a lot and gambled even more. It was said that Liam had his own seat at the bar of the The Raging Wind, the Satsapoo Tribe's ratty casino. My father said to me more than once, "That Liam is a bottom feeder. Don't go fishing anywhere he's around."

Frank and I pursued coolness with vigor. We started by sneering, then progressed to mumbling under our breath as if we were doing important calculations. We wouldn't answer direct questions or look anyone in the eye and were habitually late to every class but Ms. Swish's. We thought it cool to saunter down the hallway like we thought Miles Davis might. Today, I have no doubt that many, seeing me and Frank sauntering, thought, "Can't they get shoes that fit?"

As young philosophers and cool guys, Frank and I considered ourselves wisdom seekers. That's why we started listening to Frank's Great-Uncle Berne. Uncle Berne was dripping with wisdom. He also dripped body odor, so you couldn't get a lot of wisdom from him before you had to bolt for fresh air. Because our time with him was necessarily short, we only got snippets of wisdom and treasured them accordingly.

"You can only really know yourself," he'd say. Or, "Small things get big in a hurry." Or, "Who stole my pie?" He also said the word "enlightenment" a lot, so we had to find out what that meant. It took a long time to realize Uncle Berne didn't have a clue what he was talking about. Thankfully, I never loaned him any money.

It turns out that enlightenment is what people in Devilbridge call growing up. Frank and I figured we'd grow up no matter what happened, so it felt logical to believe that we already possessed enlightenment.

"Are you sure we're not cool already?" I asked Frank one day while we were walking down Washcon Avenue. "I mean, we're already enlightened."

"Not the same thing," Frank said. "Enlightenment is something you are. Cool is something you do."

"Cool," I said. "But if we have to do something, what is it?"

Frank answered by suddenly acting like a space robot pretending to be a human. Naturally, I fell into a jerky spasm next to him like machinery going bad.

"Why are you always upstaging me, man?" Frank would ask, in a robot voice.

"I'm not upstaging you," I'd say, sounding more like a farm hand from Alabama than spastic machinery. "I'm side-staging you." We laughed wildly and approaching people gave us wide berth.

It was around that time that we began speaking mock German, sprinkling our conversations with *umlauts* and manipulating phlegm to imitate guttural vibrato. Walking down Washcon Avenue was like being in acting class. We repeated the same sounds over and over and I suspect any authentic German observing us would have concluded we were Australians with nagging throat infections who walked funny.

Passing Elmo & Trudy's Diner once, I went slack like a drug addict in front of the entire front window section. At least a dozen people watched as Frank attempted to give me Good Samaritan assistance. It took us about ten minutes to travel fifty feet. It was our best performance of the year, and we tried repeating it again a month later. Alas, we encountered a bad audience and were shooed away by Elmo.

. . . .

"It all comes down to money" my father reminded anyone who'd listen to him. And it was true, as Frank and I well knew. Cool guys had spending money, enough to buy or do cool things. We didn't even have allowances.

One day, an excited Frank came to my house. "Guess what?" he asked.

"You have rhubarb pie?"

"No. One of my uncles gave me a tip on a job."

"A job?"

"He said they're always looking for dishwashers at the Devilbridge Hotel & Bar."

The Devilbridge Hotel & Bar had been in operation for as long as anyone could remember. It was a squat, wide building that took up half a block square on the corner of Hazeltown & Sissler. It had a two main entrances, one facing each street in case customers got lost. We walked past the hotel on our way to Smelt Field during baseball season. It exuded a sweet, sickly smell of stale beer and burnt onions. It was a close second in The Most Disgusting Stench category, the pulp mill near Piccolo winning by a wide margin.

"I called them," Frank said. They said we could come down and apply."

"We?"

"Of course we," Frank said, using his dramatic thespian voice. He focused on me with a deep look. "One cannot be cool alone, man."

. . . .

Standing on the rigid rubber mat at the Devilbridge Hotel & Bar's kitchen dishwashing station, I felt embraced by good fortune. Frank and I had been hired on the spot. We spoke with a man we never saw again. The terms were these: after a first shift together learning how to operate the Devilbridge dishwashing machine, Frank and I would then work alternating 3pm to 11pm shifts, Monday through Saturday.

The dishwashing station was as minimal as the talent it took to manage it. Fundamentally, it was an aluminum hood straddling racks of dirty dishes. When the hood was down and the GO button pushed, the dishwasher sounded like you were riding through Lil' Demon Car Wash with your windows down. The dishwasher held two racks, so that you could safely load twenty-four coffee cups and a dozen plates at a time. During our maiden voyage, I broke four cups and Frank broke three.

As Uncle Berne said, "If you survive, they let you come back the next day." We survived.

Frank and I learned quickly that by keeping the dishwashing machine crammed full of dishes, cups, and silverware, we had time to cogitate on more important thoughts, such as if Mindy, the foxy waitress, preferred boys or girls.

The technical requirements of the job were relatively easy. We piled the filled racks into the machine, then added the dishwashing liquid, a substance we referred to as Toxi-Clean, as Frank and I developed rashes on our arms that didn't fully resolve until we quit.

The dirty dishes came to us from the bar station which did double duty as the dining room station. Whenever one of the plastic bins that held the dirty dishes and glasses was full, Mindy would press a button that alerted the dishwasher. It was a little bell device that made a stinging, metallic sound. It caused me to start with shock every time I heard it, like a lab rat in a science project. The dishwasher would then retrieve the bin and take it to the dishwashing station where the magic happened.

The coolest thing about the job, other than the minimum wage money we earned, was that we were eventually allowed to take our one shift break in the Devilbridge Hotel bar. At sixteen, going into an adult drinking establishment is better than winning Wimbledon.

Broadly speaking, in Devilbridge, every tavern is a hallowed place. More sots spend their Sundays in a tavern or bar than they ever did at church. No wonder being in the Devilbridge Hotel bar felt like an achievement bestowed by God. Who cared if the place was low lit and slightly seedy or reeked of Lysol and peanuts? For Frank and me, simply being there conferred upon us a kind of spiritual worldliness. As far as we were concerned, we could have spent quality time anywhere on the planet and it wouldn't have measured up to the Devilbridge Hotel bar.

Frank was then writing a sporting column for the Demon Distributor, our high school paper, while I busied myself with eliminating "thine" from my poetry. Of course, any down-in-the-heel tavern is a potential Eden to a man with literary ambitions. Just ask any Nobel Prize winner who drank themselves to death.

It took a month of dishwashing to convince Mindy that we weren't spies in the employ of management. Eventually, she allowed us to sit at the corner table near the jukebox on Sunday nights. Sunday night was the night the Devilbridge Jazz Band played. Mindy brought us Arnold Palmers and Shirley Temples as Frank and I were allowed to enjoy the first set.

"After that," Mindy said, "you boys are going to have to skedaddle. I can make an excuse for the first set if I have to, but after that no way, Jose. That's when the heavy hitters come in." She giggled and swayed away into the edges of our fantasies where we were cool with the coolest waitress in history.

It may be a coincidence, but I grew an inch and a half over the next year, and Frank four inches. We called it "cool growth."

How do you like us now, Ms. Swish?

. . . .

The leader of the kitchen was Chef Pieburn, a man who held himself in unwarranted high esteem. He took breathing to be an opportunity to swell his chest. With a venous nose and *circonférence de grandeur*, Chef Pieburn sniffed and tasted his way around the kitchen like a police inspector. A florid, handsome man, Chef Pieburn wore a pencil thin mustache that had its own attitude. If something was wrong, he'd root it out within minutes. In Chef Pieburn's world, he was not merely the judge, he was the jury and the executioner. If you got on the wrong side of him, as Frank and I never did, he'd give you both barrels.

Carlo, the chef's number two, offered me and Frank our first experience with a yes-man in action. Carlo was a master sycophant with the mien of a debauched cherub. No one could make whining sound more pleasantly eager. He shadowed Chef Pieburn all over the place.

Once, almost tripping over Carlo, who was in the way again, the Chef shouted, "Carlo, please. Be a help, not a hurdle."

"Sorry," Carlo replied with a minion's sniffle. "I was only wanting to stir the béchamel."

Chef Pieburn never went both barrels on Carlo. That was saved for lousy short order cooks and the dishwashing lead man, Ahmed. I had no idea where Ahmed was from, only that it wasn't Devilbridge. He barely spoke English, his favorite word being "*Dondweet.*" We figured it was his native tongue, but where that was or what *Dondweet* meant we had no idea.

Ahmed said *Dondweet* all the time while instructing me and Frank, and we always gave him the same response. "Huh?"

After several shifts being instructed by Ahmed, we finally figured out that *Dondweet* meant "Don't do it." Apparently, where Ahmed came from, no one could do things better than he could. "*Dondweet*" might as well have been translated as "How could you be so stupid?" Nothing was good enough for him. No wonder he always looked like he wanted to murder someone. Frank and I decided Ahmed was in Devilbridge because he was forced to leave wherever he came from.

Then it turned out that Ahmed wasn't our supervisor at all. He was merely the day dishwasher who hung around only so he could shout "*Dondweet*" at us. One day, Carlo told Frank that Ahmed didn't work there anymore. In Frank's re-telling, Ahmed ran afoul of Chef Pieburn when he shouted "*Dondweet*," while looking in the chef's direction.

I feel obliged to state that Ahmed did teach me something important. He taught me to pile the big plates before the smaller plates before launching them into the Devilbridge Hotel's dishwashing machine, a machine of infamous ill-temperament. And Frank told me he learned from Ahmed the proper way to hold the sprayer. Life lessons, for sure. Many months later Frank said he saw Ahmed at Vander Hoek Park, shouting "*Dondweet*" at a dog.

It became progressively obvious that Carlo and Chef Pieburn were a couple. Frank was the one who confirmed it, telling me he saw them holding hands very briefly by the cooler. In Devilbridge, sexual preferences are one's own business. In fact, Devilbridge had the first gay rights parade in Greater New Rotterdam. It was on a Thursday. Seven drunken men dressed like Dolly Parton had marched around the block twice. No one batted an eye. Far from being put off by gays, Frank and I were jealous of them. They had stuff going on, we didn't.

As a matter of organization, Chef Pieburn and Carlo focused on the Devilbridge Hotel & Bar's upper end entrees, menu items like steaks and fancy salads, or fish fingers with aioli. Mindy called it "snob food." The short order cook basically did the rest. Burgers and fries, the heavy lifting. As Chef Pieburn explained it to me, a short order cook is a quantity man, whereas the chef is a quality man.

"Quantity men come and go," he said. "But quality men are hard to find." Ten years after my stint as a dishwasher, I saw Chef Pieburn and Carlo at Vander Hoek Park. It was during Demon Days. They were manning a tent serving fish fingers with aioli.

Except for the tent with dog biscuits, theirs had the longest line.

. . . .

Most short order cooks prefer to be employed for no more than a month. At least that was true at the Devilbridge Hotel & Bar. Frank and I worked with three such cooks during our brief tour of duty.

Our first short order cook was named José. José was from Mexico. A nice enough guy in his twenties, quiet, always looking over his shoulder as if afraid someone was sneaking up on him. José, sadly, was one of those people who loses a fight before it begins. You could see it in his eyes, black pits of defeat.

"Beseeching," is how Frank described Jose's look. I thought the better word was "Pleading."

José walked in a perpetual slump, his existential burden heavy upon him. Even questions like "would you like cheese or no cheese on your burger?" possessed more vigor than Jose had. But José's most serious defect wasn't emotional lack of being, it was his flatulence. As my father would have observed, José played the butt bongos big time. Major league. Tito Puente was a tyro compared to José.

"Oof, so many beans, señor," Carlo said once, waving a rag towel in front of his face in the manner of a geisha with a fan. "It is not nice for the florals."

Mindy, who wore too much eye shadow, flirted with me once. Yes, I know, Frank couldn't believe it either. Mindy had walked past my station carrying two bowls of Demon Stew, Thursday night's special. She caught my eye and held it as she slowed down to lean in toward me and whisper, "José just cut one. Pass it along." As she continued away, she turned her head to see if I appreciated how cute and naughty she was. I did.

Mindy later got a job as the weather girl on KROT, eventually becoming a TV pitch woman for various New Rotterdam enterprises such as Ford Brothers Chevrolet and Big Chair City. I believe she still waves from a float or two during New Rotterdam's annual Begonia Parade.

Chief Pieburn had a sensitive nose. He once asked me to cut back on the Toxi-Clean "before my snot turns blue." José must have turned Chef Pieburn's nose blue, because in less than two weeks, Chef Pieburn fired him for excessive butt bongoing.

"What did he expect me to do?" he said to Carlo, his jowls shaking with supervisory distaste. "No kitchen I command shall stink like that," he said. "I swear on my mother's name, may she rest in eternal peace."

"Mama was a saint," said Carlo, and they gave each other goo eyes.

Thereafter, until another short-order cook could be found, Carlo took over José's station. I was told to spray the air with a disinfectant occasionally for the remainder of Jose's final shift, and we all went back to work in a more environmentally protected atmosphere.

Two days later I arrived for my shift and found a new short order cook. His name was Toby. I was first impressed by his t-shirt. On the front were two beer mugs leaning into each other, and on the back was stenciled DEVILBRIDGE USA." Toby might have been forty, or sixty, or twenty-five. He looked like he slept in a ditch. The boots he wore were at least three sizes too big. Apparently, the list of available short order cooks in the Devilbridge area had grown thin that week.

Toby mumbled to himself constantly, and occasionally got angry at someone who wasn't there. Everyone tried their best to avoid him. On his third day, Toby was caught by Carlo in the freezer snuggling up to a bottle of vodka. Chef Pieburn was summoned and Toby was shuffled back to the bottom of the of available short order cook list.

Frank had a better experience with Toby than I did, as Toby made Frank a Crab Louie. Neither of us had ever heard of a Crab Louie. Actually, Toby made Frank two Crab Louies, since Frank slipped on something while carrying the first one, dumping Toby's masterpiece across the floor. After that, Chef Pieburn gave us a new job. He called it "swabbing the deck."

"Tell your buddy, too," he told Frank. "What you do, he does." For reasons that remained hidden to Frank, Carlo found that an extremely funny comment.

"You too much, Jonnie," Frank said Carlo said.

"I think I'm just enough," Chef Pieburn replied with a wink. Carlo walked over to him and sweetly brushed away some flour from Chef Pieburn's lapel.

....

Before one shift, my mother slathered my arms with cortisone cream and insisted I wear one of my father's long sleeve shirts as protection against Toxi-Clean. I arrived at the hotel a few minutes early so I could wash off the cortisone. I noticed a tallish, slender man in his mid-twenties at the short order station. I was stopped in my tracks. He was the coolest guy I'd ever seen.

His name was Rondo, and Rondo was a picture of equipoise. Nothing about him was out of place. As handsome as handsome can be, he moved as if propelled by inner music. Six feet tall or more, I guessed Rondo to weigh as much as my sister, a hundred and seventy pounds. ("Give or take a few lunches," as my father would say.)

Mindy's response to seeing Rondo was "God, what a hunk." She repeated it even when shaking his hand hello. I can't count the number of times Mindy embarrassed herself in front of Rondo. Of course, Rondo was a gentleman and didn't give her the time of day.

Rondo also impressed Chef Pieburn and Carlo. Carlo attempted to hide his attraction to Rondo in front of Chef Pieburn, but Chef Pieburn didn't reciprocate. He started calling Rondo "Adonis." Every time he said it, he'd look to Carlo and they'd both purse their lips in weird ways, indicating private protocols that ought to remain private.

Whenever Rondo moved, Chef Pieburn and Carlo reacted as if they were connected to him by strings of desire. When Rondo reached up to get a plate from the overhead storage area, allowing his t-shirt to ride up, Carlo would twist himself so that he was not merely as low as he could go, but almost upside down. If Rondo bent to change the garbage liner, Chef Pieburn would lean in for a peek. It wasn't hard for me and Frank to appreciate why they drooled over him. Rondo moved like a dancer, every inch of him rhythmic and fine. Indeed, Frank and I both agreed that Rondo was a major looker. If you were a gay guy, Rondo's pinup picture might be worth good money.

Rondo was also a quick and efficient short order cook, and he always smelled as good as he looked. Importantly, as Mindy observed to Carlo, Rondo neither drank nor cut the cheese. They both agreed that in the short order cook world, Rondo was as close to perfection as could be fathomed.

Frank had our first conversation with Rondo. Here's how Frank relayed it to me:

Frank: "You're Rondo, right?"

Rondo: "That's what my license says." (Rondo's light laugh was a light shining into eternity. It seemed always followed by a Carlo coo.)

Frank: "So, you cook, huh?"

Rondo: "Yeah, for now. Building a nest egg for my next gig."

Frank: "Next gig?"

Rondo: "Yeah, my next tour."

Frank: "You tour?"

Rondo: "I'm a drummer, in real life." (Light laugh, followed by coo.)

Frank: "That's cool."

Rondo: "Yeah, I've played with a bunch of bands. I'm with The Lesions now, but we're taking a break because our lead singer joined the Army."

Frank: "That's cool."

After Frank told me about his conversation with Rondo, I knew I'd have to have one too. This is how my conversation with Rondo went.

Me: "Frank said you played drums."

Rondo: "Yeah. And I dance too."

Me: "Cool."

Rondo: "Yeah, it is."

Neither Frank nor I had heard of The Lesions, and we certainly had never seen Rondo dance. We weren't rock groupies, just Devilbridge teenagers seeking coolness, and Rondo was without question the coolest guy we'd ever seen. His coolness was on a par with Ms. Swish. We imagined Rondo on the big screen, dancing around the world arm-in-arm with Ms. Swish. Here they are in Morocco, here in St. Tropez. Say, isn't that Rondo and Ms. Swish on the red carpet at the Oscars?

Alas, we were not on the red carpet, but astride industrial rubber mats that I, for one, was always tripping over.

It was our first lesson from the cool school of hard knocks. Rondo and Ms. Swish had what it took. We didn't.

. . . .

Rondo was a man of routine. He arrived exactly ten minutes before his shift each day, always wearing a black t-shirt with faded blue jeans, both shoes and socks were black. His hair was black, even blacker than my sister's during her Goth phase. If someone mentioned how black his hair was, he'd shoot them with his finger and smile. His t-shirts fit him perfectly and Mindy figured Rondo knew his way around a washing machine. Carlo told her he thought Rondo used an expensive lilac-scented fabric softener.

A wry, knowing look lingered about him always. A worldly cynicism. He looked like the Steve McQueen of my mother's movie poster that went missing a few years ago. My father hated Steve McQueen.

"What kind of name is McQueen?" he'd thunder.

"Hush yourself," my mother would caution. "You're speaking of royalty."

Rondo was so cool that Frank and I talked about him all the time. "His hair. How does he get his hair to do that?" I asked Frank.

"Some people just wake up with hair like that," Frank said. "The lucky ones."

Indeed, Rondo's hair was no less than an artwork. Did he use hair products? Cool gel?

"I'll bet he has a hair stylist," I said.

"Are those real Levis or Berg Emporium knockoffs?" Frank wondered.

"Look like the real thing to me," I said. We had both been raised to wear Lees like our fathers. Steve McQueen was probably a Levis man like Rondo. Goodbye, Lees. "And his t-shirts. How many t-shirts do you have? I only have three and my sister stole one of them." While Frank thought about that, I added, "Rondo must have a dozen. They're all so....black."

One afternoon, on my day off, I was at the Washcon Mall. Passing the Outrageous Rag Co.'s display window, I saw t-shirts exactly like the one's Rondo wore. I couldn't believe it. I went in and found piles of them, all colors, all sizes. The tags indicated that they were made in China from recycled materials. The Outrageous Rag Co.s own label. $1.99 each. I bought four black ones, two smalls for me, and, figuring Frank would want two, mediums for him. By the time I left the Mall, I felt as buoyant as my mother re-watching "Bullitt."

"Looks like someone shops at Outrageous Rag," Rondo said to me when I showed up at my dishwashing station the next day. He made it sound like a compliment.

"Yeah," I said leaning against the dishwasher like it was an expensive car. "I like their stuff."

Rondo looked me up and down, nodded with approval.

It was a tender moment for me. A direct interaction with cool.

. . . .

The Devilbridge Hotel & Bar's bar was dismal, a dive. When the lights were on, a rare occurrence, you could see spider webs lined along the ceiling. When you left it, you invariably discovered dust had settled on your arm. As much as Mindy swept and cleaned, the bar remained a pig sty where no one in their right mind would want to drink. Luckily, among those not in their right mind are jazz fans. A small pack of them arrived each Sunday night to enjoy jazz, along with the smell of stale peanuts. And the reason they came was The Devilbridge Jazz Band, a collection of bebop veterans whose goatees dripped cool as much as they did beer.

One Sunday night, Frank and I sat listening to the band's first set in the hotel bar. The stage was small, taking up only a corner of the room. We'd been dishwashing in the hotel kitchen for almost two months at this point, already veterans, feeling like old timers. It was then our third Sunday in the bar.

No one noticed us as we took our table near the back. We referred to it as "our" table, as if we were regulars. It was next to the curtain folds which provided a decent hiding place if the wrong people came into the place. Wrong people such as our parents, or Fran the Nag.

The Devilbridge Jazz Band was halfway through "Polka Dots and Moonbeams" when Frank first saw Rondo.

"Hey, that's Rondo, right?"

He pointed to a table up by the band. Yes, indeed, it was Rondo I confirmed. Frank waved, but Rondo didn't see us. His head was down, grooving to the music.

"He's got the same jazz sway as Ms. Swish does," I noted.

"No kidding," said Frank. "You're exactly right."

"Cool," I said to myself. My teen ego always swelled a bit after Frank agreed with me.

Jazz aficionados transport themselves to other realms of consciousness, such as places that have polka dots and moonbeams. In other words, places unlike Devilbridge. I'd never seen a polka dot in Devilbridge, let alone a moonbeam. Lots of soot and mold, but no moonbeams.

A spray of Rondo's black hair hung over his brow as he drummed his fingers on the table. It matched his black t-shirt and Levi's. From the pictures I've seen of James Dean, another of my mother's favorites, Rondo easily could have been standing next to him. A pal of James Dean's. And just as James Dean could never die, Rondo couldn't either. Cool is not bounded by time. Like eternity, cool just is.

About fifteen jazz fans were scatted around a room that might hold fifty when the fire marshal wasn't around. Mindy, fixated on Rondo, avoided her customers until they yelled for her attention. Every time he took a sip of his beer, she attended his table immediately to ask if he wanted a refill. Rondo always shook his head, no. He had jazz on his mind, not Mindy.

In the darkened room, the lights behind the bar cast a pleasant light. With Rondo, it gave him the aura of a cool prince. As the band played, Rondo's black hair bounced to the music. His black shoes tapped. From top to bottom he was in the throes of being cool. His entire being bopped to the music. And Frank and

I bopped with him, following the master by drumming our fingers on our table. But we sucked, and after Mindy threw us a nasty look, we stopped.

"Oh, man, maybe they'll ask Rondo to play with them," I said. Frank saw the hope in my eyes and matched them.

"That would be beyond cool," he said, ratcheting up the expectation. "The coolest."

We knew that the Devilbridge Jazz Band occasionally invited musicians up to join them on stage. We'd seen that happen before when a groovy cat was digging the music and the leader of the Devilbridge Jazz Band, the trombonist, whose name was Early Reiser, invited the cat to join them. His name was Bobo, and Bobo played a mean blues harp. But Bobo wasn't nearly as cool as Rondo was. No doubt, Rondo would blow the Devilbridge Jazz Band off the stage. We could hardly wait. For his part, Rondo was hammering on his table as if he were Gene Krupa.

· · · · · · · ·

Just then, the crowd of patrons turned their attention to the entryway with a buzz of excitement. I pulled the curtain aside and looked. Frank craned his neck and looked too. Was it Bobo? No, it was not Bobo. It was the glorious Ms. Swish. And Ms. Swish was dressed to kill.

She strode the length of the room, headed toward the stage, wearing a grand red ankle-length sleeveless gown, slitted at the leg all the way until further would have been illegal. She was stunning and she knew it. Each patron gasped in turn as she passed them.

They were not the only ones in shock. Mindy leaned against the bar as if she'd been shot. She recovered enough to begin throwing evil eye darts at Ms. Swish. My father told me that there is no fury equal to a woman's. I never knew what he meant until I saw Mindy in that moment. If Mindy and Ms. Swish had just then gotten into a cat fight, my money would be on Ms. Swish. Those legs could kill a crocodile.

And then the unbelievable happened.

Rondo rose from his table, a half-rise, hinting a gentlemanly bow. His eyes went to Ms. Swish. As she arrived at his table, he bade her to sit. She did.

I felt like an extra in one of my mother's old movies. Bogie and Bacall. My jaw dropped, I lost my gum.

Frank turned. I looked at him. We both mouthed, "Wha?"

"Ms. Swish is with Rondo." Frank gasped.

"Wha?"

We watched Rondo and Ms. Swish as they nodded instead of spoke. Language for them was more than words, it was something erupting from deep chasms of cool. It was like watching God transmit the truths to Moses.

Rondo and Ms. Swish grooved to the music because that's what you do when you're the coolest things ever. After the tune the Devilbridge Jazz Band finished, Early Reiser said, "And now we'd like to play a classic, a favorite of ours. Maybe it's a favorite of yours, too. It's called 'Jeru.'"

Frank and I looked at each other and mouthed in silent unison, "Wha?." It was Jeru. Cool Jazz and Devilbridge High School English in the same moment. Wha?

We saw Rondo and Ms. Switch look to each other and mouth, "Jeru," Frank and I looked at each other and mouthed "Jeru." Mindy mouthed, "Who's Jeru?"

Our first instinct was to stand and break into wild applause, but knew we shouldn't. For starters, Mindy might not appreciate it, and ask us to leave. But being asked to leave in the middle of a cool fest wasn't happening, so we sat still. We'd washed too many dishes not to feel entitled to a night out in cool town. Even so, the uncool should never outshine the cool, so our instincts kept us in our seats. We were meant only to be witness to the moment. Acolytes and worshippers from afar.

The band began its intro to the tune Frank and I knew so well. Jeru. Sweet, fun, cool Jeru. Ms. Swish had said once in class that Jeru's swing "swang in the rain." How cool is that?

"He's up," said Frank, elbowing me.

Rondo rose and offered his hand to Ms. Swish. Ms. Swish took Rondo's hand and together they strode to the center of the the dance floor. It was a small dance floor and no one else was on it. That was a good thing because it seemed to us that Rondo and Ms. Swish intended to use every square inch. How cool they were. How glorious and cool.

. . . .

As much as Frank and I worshipped Rondo and Ms. Swish, we were new to the worshipping game so couldn't have know that one of the first rules of hero worship is "Be Prepared to Be Heart Broken."

The truth hit us hard. For far from being Fred Astaire and Ginger Rogers, Rondo and Ms. Swish revealed themselves to be practitioners of the Danse Macabre. For starters, Rondo's arms and legs sputtered all over the place. He was like a machine gone amok, a metronome gone mad. He herked and jerked and swiveled like a broken slinky. In one moment he strutted, another moment he looked like he was about to take a dump. Let me tell you, it's difficult to watch your hero while he hunches like a dog scratching fleas.

Meanwhile, Ms. Swish had gone to the middle of the dance floor to begin twirling like a dervish. That was it. She simply spun in the middle of the floor like a physics experiment gone wrong. How Ms. Swish didn't get dizzy and throw up all over Rondo, I'll never know. I once saw Fran the Nag polka dancing at a Lutheran Bingo Festival and, believe me, Rondo and Ms. Swish were worse. Far, far worse.

Frank and I were undone. What was happening? I was so disillusioned that I hung my head in shame. We couldn't look at each other. Frank stared straight ahead, his face cradled by his hands, muttering, "Oh, my God. Oh, my God."

On stage, Early Reiser's eyes grew as fat as his balloon cheeks. The rest of the band noticed the dancing demons, too. They giggled to each other, rolled their eyes, made their syncopations more robust, so as to mimic Rondo's insane stomping and occasional arm thrusts. One arm thrust caused Frank to moan, "Oh no. Rondo's a Nazi."

"Ms. Swish thinks she's a corkscrew," I stammered.

Only Mindy seemed pleased. I have never seen anyone enjoy hatred so much.

Frank and I could not speak. We were mute, silenced by the instant destruction of our cool dreams. The only comparable feeling I can conjure is when I was in grade school and Timmy Showalter told me that Santa was his really his father. It felt like a stab to the heart of the mind. The unmasking of a lie.

Rondo and Ms. Swish, were not only un-cool, they possibly had brain disease. Had we deceived ourselves, or had Rondo and Ms. Swish deceived us? I began to wonder if my father hadn't been right all along. The world was indeed out to get me.

Frank and I didn't finish our Arnold Palmers. We just slunk out the door of the Devilbridge Hotel's bar feeling our parents were cooler than Rondo and Ms. Swish, an indication of the depth of our depression. It isn't natural for sixteen year olds to think their parents cool. Clearly the planets had misaligned. And just like that, the salad days of Rondo and Ms. Swish were gone. Trashed on the Devilbridge Hotel & Bar's dance floor.

We did not speak while walking home until Frank said, "No wonder we never heard of the Lesions."

· · · · · · · ·

Frank and I quit our jobs as dishwashers the very next day. We phoned our resignation in, not being able to face Chef Pieburn, Carlo, or Mindy in person. We certainly could not face Rondo. It was enough that we'd have to see Ms. Swish. We prayed she had not seen us.

After a short time, Frank and I realized we had learned an important lesson from our time washing dishes at the Devilbridge Hotel & Bar. We learned that coolness is in the mind of the beholder. That it is transitory, comes and goes with the wind. You can't count on it, like you can a pal. Coolness lives by a different code, one we clearly did not know.

Frank and I moved on with life as young people do after any tragedy. Though we no longer had paying gigs, we had learned that money has nothing to do with being cool. In fact, we decided that cool was for chumps. Naturally, not wishing to be chumps, we determined to become nihilists. But we weren't very good nihilists, and decided to perk ourselves up by trying out for the Devilbridge High fall term production of "Hair."

I didn't make the first cut and Frank ended up as an extra in a wig. Ms. Swish was the director.

Go, Demons.

Halvard Sees The World

They sat beneath Saul's Elm in New Rotterdam's Occidental Park. It was a magnificent tree named after the man who had paid good money to plant it and name it after himself. Most observant New Rotterdam tourists can identify two landmarks after having visited the City of Fair Fortune: Saul's Elm and The Pink Leopard Car Wash sign.

It was a beautiful Sunday afternoon in late May. The chill that normally swept in with the northwest wind was absent, perfect weather for two high school seniors not yet adults but old enough to think themselves so. Halvard and Berthe were picnicking while overlooking Inauguration Bay. He was joining the Navy and she was seeing him off like a proper New Rotterdam lady would.

Halvard's buddies were at Smelt Field watching baseball. They knew a guy who'd buy them beer. Halvard was jealous of them, wishing he were watching the Smelt lose again instead of sitting on the picnic blanket Berthe won last year at St. Olaf's Lutheran's Thor Heyerdahl Day raffle. It was a replica of the Norwegian flag.

From the soft grass where Berthe and Halvard sat, they saw the greater part of Inauguration Bay fanned out before them, featuring the long nose of Sat's Spit.

A photo of Saul's Elm is always featured on the front of the New Rotterdam Chamber of Commerce annual brochure. One still hangs opposite the cash register at Saul's Elm Cafe on East Washcon, next to the wrecking yard.

"Look at all those empty ships," Halvard said, his finger tracing the horizon where six ships were variously moored in the wide bay. He found the ships fascinating, they connected New Rotterdam to the world, and Halvard's most fervent wish was to see the world.

"How do you know they're empty?" Berthe asked.

"From how high they sit above the waterline. That means they're empty. Haven't been loaded yet."

Berthe tuned out, two things she didn't care about were ships and baseball. She didn't care about football either, but Halvard didn't like football so it never came up. Berthe unloaded from her mother's antique picnic basket a plate of sardine sandwiches with their crusts removed.

Among St. Olaf's parishioners Berthe was known for three things: the excellence of her pickled sardine sandwiches, her rhubarb pie, and the grandeur of her breasts. Many a St. Olaf geezer suffered from irritable wife syndrome after having lingered a bit too long near Berthe's pickled sardines.

"There's nothing she can do about it," Berthe's mother said once to Signe Haugen, feeling the need to defend her daughter's breast size because Lars Haugen was a drooling fool. "God made her the way she is, Signe, and that should be good enough for any Lutheran, even you."

Halvard leaned back on his elbows and looked up at Berthe. "Yeah, you load a ship up to its marks," he said, leaning to his side and plucking a long blade of grass. He put it in his mouth and let it dangle. "More than that and and it'll sink," he said like he knew what he was talking about. Halvard and most of his friends had longshoremen as fathers. Talking like he knew what he was talking about was second nature.

Berthe's second nature was not to listen. She did listen, but only if was more interesting than what she was thinking. For this reason, she'd become an interrupter, an incessant editor of conversation. Halvard's father once observed, "The only silence Berthe likes is someone else's."

"So, the Navy?" Berthe said, her tone suggesting an error in judgment. She handed Halvard a sardine sandwich, and when she caught Halvard's eye, he noticed hers had narrowed. Once, when he'd had more than his share of beer, Halvard's father said, "When that girl narrows her eyes, the future should beware."

A small piece of sardine fell from a sandwich and Berthe caught it like a bird of prey handling a field mouse. Berthe examined the piece of sardine and, determining it to be food, popped it into her mouth. She swallowed it in one gulp, her eyes widening at Halvard's. Halvard wondered if she expected applause.

Halvard nodded. Halvard was constant nodder. His nodding made people think he already knew what they were about to say. He came to nodding honestly. His father was a nodder, too. Halvard's mother thought it was cute when Halvard was young. "You two are so cute," she would say. Later, after he and his dad weren't so cute, she'd say, "What's with you two bobbleheads?"

Since Halvard decided to join the Navy, he'd been nodding twice as much as usual. People passing him on the sidewalk thought him the most agreeable young man in New Rotterdam.

. . . .

Is there a better way to see the world than to join the Navy? His father had agreed as they signed the enlistment papers, allowing seventeen-year-old Halvard to join. "You can't see the world from a foxhole," his father had cautioned. But Halvard needed no persuasion not to join the Army. Marching around a barracks until it's time to go get killed didn't appeal to him one bit. And the Air Force meant planes. Halvard knew you can't see shit from a plane because two summers previously he had flown to Boise for a cousin's wedding and it was shit all the way there. When someone suggested the Coast Guard, Halvard grew testy. "I don't want to see what I can already see from Saul's Elm," he snarled. "I want to see the world."

The world. The places you can't see from the borders of New Rotterdam. A lot of people thought that meant Seattle, just an hours drive away. As far as Halvard was concerned, Seattle was an expensive New Rotterdam with worse traffic. If the world beyond meant Seattle, why leave New Rotterdam at all? Hell, you can drive to Seattle for lunch. Same weather, same attitude, same chilly demeanor.

Halvard wanted to experience the larger world. He didn't want to just look at it from under Saul's pretty elm. He wanted something different, something not the same.

"Really? Why? Are you in love with ocean water?" Berthe said, when Halvard told her he was joining the Navy. "My father said everyone knows the ocean is an evil mistress."

They sat in silence for a couple of minutes. Berthe lowered herself sideways, onto a one elbow. With her free hand she smoothed the Norwegian flag blanket while Halvard imagined himself lounging outside a bar in Marseilles with Tom Cruise. Him and Tom, checking out the ladies.

Halvard spoke. "My dad says it makes sense. Serve my country. Maybe learn a skill. Earn some money. Like any job, except you also get to see the world." Berthe stayed silent. Halvard didn't want to attend this picnic with Berthe but his mother had told him that Berthe had gone to a lot of trouble to do something for him. "Would it kill you to be nice to her for an hour?" Halvard's mother said. "You two took first communion together."

To Halvard, Berthe might be his co-communicant in Christ, but there's a limit to what a man can do. She'd been telling people she was his girlfriend since they were in sixth grade. Born a week apart, Berthe being the elder, they'd known each other their entire lives. Berthe told him that being born in the same week was a sign of destiny. Berthe often talked like this. Sometimes she'd add words like "fate" and "kismet" and go on about how the universe was aligning just right for her. For her and Halvard.

Everyone agreed that Berthe was quite pretty. "For a big girl, she's a hell of a looker," said Andy Vanderhoef, who had all kinds of girlfriends so knew what he was talking about.

Halvard never thought of Berthe as being fat. He thought of her as pretty, mouthy, and pushy. Just like her mother.

Halvard's father, generally in control of the remote, would routinely raise the volume when Berthe was around. Even then, his personal best was nine minutes in the same room with Berthe

In their freshmen year at The Wood Academy Halvard had given Berthe his St. Olaf's pin. Why? He did not know. Everyone else was doing it, so he thought he'd do it too. He knew instantly he'd erred. But it could not be undone. As his father advised, "When you do something, do it good. It's really expensive to fix bad." Halvard was afraid Berthe might be too expensive to fix.

When you asked Berthe what she liked, Berthe would tell you what she didn't like. Her favorite topics were food she wouldn't eat on a bet and why stupid people always made her late. Her most annoying habit was being a Facebook addict. Halvard's father wouldn't allow Facebook in his home, having proclaimed it too human for his tastes.

Halvard eyed Berthe in the shade of Saul's Elm. Her large breasts, her wide and eager face, her pretty mouth. She laughed to see him looking at her, and adopted a coquette pose. She allowed her jaw to open seductively, as if anticipating grapes.

Halvard's father once said she could swallow a house. "That girl eats like a pig. If she keeps it up, she'll be as big as her mother."

Halvard's looked up into the leafy bower of Saul's Elm. Tomorrow, after Berthe dropped him off at the Amtrak station, he might never see her again. He could hardly wait. I will be a man of the world, he told himself. Who knows what will happen to me? Which oceans will I cross? In what port cities will I eat and drink and be merry? On what foreign streets shall I stumble out of bars, singing and dancing? And who will be my compatriots? Who will be my pals? More importantly, who will be my girls in every port? Not Berthe, that's for sure. Berthe will be here in New Rotterdam, constantly harassed by St. Olaf's old fools. Berthe, the drooler's dream girl. A life of leftover sardine sandwiches.

"What do you think it will be like?" Berthe asked. "The Navy, I mean." Another clump of sardine fell, it landed onto her lap. She picked it up, balancing it between two fingers, examining it like an irritable queen. If the sardine weren't already dead, Halvard might have worried for its head.

"Fun, I hope." Halvard smiled, beginning a nod.

Berthe was like every New Rotterdam woman he knew. His mother, his aunts, his sister, his teachers, all shared one common trait: you did what they said or else. Halvard's father said that since someone had to be in charge, God created Norwegian women. "He probably didn't want to waste anyone's time," he said.

"I'll miss you, Halvard," Berthe said, a tear forming.

Halvard, in full nod, said, "I'll write."

"You promise?"

"Of course I promise," he said.

Berthe leaned into Halvard, pinning his arm with a breast while clutching him with both hands.

"All the time?"

"Of course," he lied. "Why wouldn't I?"

. . . .

Under the great domed hall and redwood beams of San Diego's Sante Fe Station, from different directions, three figures merged at a brightly colored ceramic tile wall. Attracted by the lostness of their auras, and a mutual sense of being awestruck by the size of the the building they were wandering through, they recognized each other at once. They were each Navy recruits on their way to Boot Camp. They introduced themselves and felt an immediate bond. We're all in this together, right?

Wilson was a black guy from Detroit. Halvard was Halvard, a white guy from New Rotterdam. Scooter was another white guy from someplace in Alabama. His accent was so thick Halvard couldn't understand a word.

"Are you going to Navy Boot Camp?" Halvard asked Scooter.

Scooter said something that had very long vowels in it. He carried a small toiletry case just as Halvard and Wilson did. Recruiters had told them, "don't worry, they'll take care of everything else." It was somehow comforting to Halvard to think his and Scooter's recruiters were on the same page. The same team.

"War yell frame?" Scooter said.

"Huh?" Harvard replied.

"Ah sawed, war yell frame?"

Halvard, bred to be mannerly, as nice as possible in any given circumstance, said, "I'm sorry, I don't speak, uh...your language."

They all sat on beautiful, well-worn wooden terminal seats. To Halvard they looked like the pews at St. Olaf's, except more ornate. Polished by wear, they looked revered, rich with history. World history.

Wilson said, "He wants to know where you're from."

Harvard told them he was from New Rotterdam, which neither Scooter nor Wilson had heard of. Not surprising, thought Halvard. Why would anyone want to know about New Rotterdam? "It's about an hour from of Seattle," he said.

A pale, thin-chested kid approached and stood staring at them for awhile until Wilson asked him, "Boot Camp?"

The kid said, "Navy."

"Us, too," said Wilson, and the kid sat down across from them on a facing pew, looking even more lost than the rest of them. Wilson immediately nicknamed him Wrapper because he had a gum wrapper stuck to the back of his head. Wrapper was from a small town in eastern Minnesota.

"I knew a Halvard once," Wrapper said. "I think he was the cousin of someone." After Halvard explained that his name was

Norwegian, Wrapper said, "Most everyone I know is Swedish, but you know how us Northern types are," he said. "We sleep around."

After a short time giving each other the once over, passing along the small bits of personal details that feed fledgling friendships, they all agreed they didn't know what to do next. Ok, we're at the San Diego train station, now what? They'd been told to be in front of the Naval Recruitment Center in San Diego the following morning at 7am. Until then they were on their own. And like every generation of Navy recruits who found themselves in the company of other Navy recruits just as lost as they are, they formed an immediate, life-lasting bond. Each of them officially a member of that ancient, proud seagoing brotherhood; that is, sailors on the prowl.

Each had joined the Navy for the same reason; that is, none could think of anything better to do. Options at home were limited.

In Halvard's case, it made sense to free himself from Berthe's dreams of foreverness. Even if he did get stuck with her, didn't he need to see the world first? Why sign up for foreverness when you haven't yet done anything?

At the train station, as he was leaving New Rotterdam, his father had said, "Remember, don't be a hurry to mess things up. That'll happen anyway."

Scooter spoke, and only Wilson could understand him. "He says he's from a poor town." According to Wilson, Scooter's high school occupational counselor told him his best future was as a drywall installer. But that was only because Scooter's father was a drywaller. Scooter hated drywall even more than he hated his father. Seeing no other way out, Scooter tried to join the Marines.

Scooter, at 5'4" tall, was also undernourished, at least that's what the Marine recruiter told him, sending him to the Navy next door. The Navy made sure he had a heart beat, then signed him up.

Wrapper, who loved his new name, told them that he was forced to join the Navy by his old man who made a deal with a judge. Wrapper described himself as a party animal. "Guess I was a bad boy," he said, exhibiting pride.

Wilson didn't say why he joined, except to say, "Nothing better goin' on."

"Whed gwandue?" Scooter wanted to know.

"Good question," Wilson said, "We gotta find someplace to stay."

Halvard agreed. "Yeah, but where?"

"How much money you got?" Wilson said, looking at Scooter.

"Fitty," Scooter said, pulling five crinkled bills out of his pocket, one of which was torn in half.

Wrapper was next. "My aunt gave me a hundred. It's in my shoe."

Halvard, who had five twenties in his wallet, and five more in his shoe, didn't want to be pegged as the wealthy one, so he said a hundred too.

Wilson said, "A cabbie'll know. Where us boot camp guys stay."

Halvard was the first to nod with agreement, and the last to stop.

The cabbie's name was Ezekial, a Rastafasarian. Ezekiel took them on a thirty minute ride to a ten minute destination. Wilson figured it out.

"Didn't we just pass that group of homeless people?" he asked Ezekiel from the front seat. Wilson said he always rode shotgun and no one disputed it.

"How can you tell?" asked Wrapper, leaning forward from the back seat to perch his chin between Wilson and Ezekial.

"How many homeless people you see wearing LeBron gear?" Wilson said. "We passed that guy twenty minutes ago. He was leanin' on the same car."

"No prob, brother," Ezikiel said, pulling to the curb in front of the Lincoln Hotel. "We there."

Ezekial sped away and the recruits stood in front of the Lincoln Hotel, taking it in. It wasn't breathtaking, just a good idea to take a deep breath before entering. They rang the bell, as the Lincoln Hotel did not let just anyone in. They heard a buzz and then the door unlock. Wilson confidently entered and the others followed. In the small anteroom were two chairs, a geezer seated in each inhaling the stale odor of camphor.

Halvard's first impression was the Lincoln Hotel needed a good steam cleaning. Scooter fingered some green mold on a window frame and sniffed it. "Jest lack Pointy Fred," he said, making a face, perhaps to mimic Pointy Fred?

. . . .

The Lincoln Hotel's desk clerk wore a sleeve of tattoos on both arms. He said, "Boot Camp, right?"

The desk clerk leaned one arm across the leatherette sign-in pad, like he was about to challenge Wilson to an arm wrestle. "See this one?" He pointed to a tattoo of a slinky pinup girl wearing a sailor's cap. "I got this one the day before I showed up down there."

"Down where?" Wilson asked.

"At Boot Camp, where do you think? Same damn place you guys are headed."

"How'd you know that's where we're going?" Wrapper asked, edging next to Wilson.

The clerk snickered in the way Berthe's uncle Lars did. Lars only came to New Rotterdam once every few years in order to borrow money from his brother that he never paid back. Berthe's father called him Lars from Mars. Halvard had only seen Uncle Lars once, and he looked a whole lot like the Lincoln Hotel clerk.

"Your name isn't Lars, is it?" Harvard asked.

"Lars? I look like a Lars to you?"

"Well, yeah, sort of," Halvard said. "You remind me of someone's uncle."

"Well, you're as wrong as shit. Christian name is Charles. Hell, Lars ain't even Christian, is it? It's pagan or something. Lots of pagans around here."

"Shawls," said Scooter.

Charles looked at Scooter hard over his cheaters, then said, "Why don't you boys call me what everyone else around here calls me..."

A faint voice from the foyer said, "asshole."

Charles chuckled and waved the faint voice away. "Why don't you just call me Chuck. Everyone calls me Chuck." With that, Chuck gave the new recruits the full tour of his right arm.

"This one I got in in England." He pointed to a pinup girl on his right forearm. "She had a sash across her lower parts that said, "Fuck the French," but I had to change that. You can almost still see the "Fuck" under that rose in the middle, the big one. And these three I got when I was in the Philippines. Missed a ship because of this one here." He pointed at a curvy girl wearing a bikini, a banner over her spelling out "Mamie."

Halvard hadn't thought of getting a tattoo. Lots of guys were getting tattoos these days in New Rotterdam. Girls too. It never made much sense to Halvard, inking yourself forever. What happens if you change your mind? Mess up once, mess up forever. Halvard didn't want to mess up forever, he just wanted to see the world.

Wilson said," One room, four beds."

Chuck explained that he'd have to bring in two folding beds, but they were just as good as the two beds that didn't fold.

"How much extra?" Wilson asked.

It was a question none of the others would have asked because none had rented a room before. Wilson was obviously the man. If they'd suddenly held an election, he would have won unanimously. Wilson had the kind of attitude that got you what you needed. And they all needed to get into boot camp without any problems. They each gave Wilson some money and Wilson and Chuck conducted business as Halvard looked around the hotel lobby.

The two old men looked dead in their chairs. Halvard couldn't determine which one opined that Chuck was an asshole. The chairs also looked dead. Brown and stained, they held their loads unevenly. Whatever sturdiness they possessed was the result of having been compressed so long. They were like stones you can squeeze nothing more from.

Wallpaper peelings draped from the walls, the paper itself a filthy green aligned with gray stripes. The woodwork, even filthier, surrounded two dirty windows on either side of twin doors, doors that kept the Lincoln Hotel safe from its neighbors. Halvard drew a finger across the woodwork. He examined it briefly before showing it to the others, like a scientist proving grime exists.

Scooter said, "Mah lard, thad sump natty crip."

Wrapper said, "I know."

How cool is that? thought Halvard. Seeing the world includes saying "I know," to someone you don't even understand. People from different places seeing the world together, just differently.

The door buzzer sounded. Someone wanted in. Chuck reached under the desk and they heard the click again and the door opened. A tall red haired woman appeared, leading a scrawny, older man who looked like Mr. Schadt, Halvard's chemistry teacher at The Wood Academy.

"Chuck, sweetie. 304, half hour," she said commandingly. She turned to the scrawny man. "Half an hour good enough for you, honey?"

Mr. Schadt's *doppelgänger* followed the woman as she headed up the stairs. He kept his head down the entire time. The woman stopped once and looked back at Mr. Schadt. She didn't seem happy about Mr. Schadt. She looked like Berthe after one too many milkshakes.

After Chuck had returned from going upstairs to "get those fucking cots," Wilson got the room key. The foursome walked up two flights of stairs to Room 305. They walked into the hallway. Down the hall stood the woman and Mr. Schadt. She was fumbling with her door key as Mr. Schadt busied himself by feeling her up.

Scooter heehawed and said (as Wilson translated), "He's puckering the fruit."

"Hold on, old timer," the woman said to Mr. Schadt. "Plenty of time. Plenty of time," as Mr. Schadt shoved his bald head into her armpits.

Room 305 had two single beds and two cots shoehorned into Room 305's small square. Wrapper said he thought it looked like a jail cell, but then admitted he'd never seen a jail cell. Halvard, noticing the room had the same green wallpaper as the foyer, said, "If it is a jail cell, it needs new wallpaper."

Wilson said, "This one's mine," and tossed himself onto one of the single beds.

Halvard started to move toward the other single bed, but Scooter got to it first. He fell back onto it, raised his legs, and loudly broke wind. Halvard figured that was how Alabamans claimed dibs. Scooter grinned like he'd won something.

Wrapper and Halvard looked at each other, Halvard making a magnanimous bow. "Your choice, Wrapper. They both look equally bad."

"In that case," Wrapper said, "I'll take the one with a view." He threw his small bag on the cot next to the window. "Boy, great view," he said looking out, kneeling on the cot.

All of them came to the window and peered out at a cement wall.

"I don't think this is jail," Wrapper said. "I think it's prison."

But Wilson seemed to feel right at home. "Fair crib," he said. "Reminds me of my hood, little bit."

Scooter said "igloo," which Wilson translated as, "It'll do."

Halvard reckoned that the Lincoln Hotel might be usual in Detroit, or fancy in Alabama, but in New Rotterdam, it would be shuttered because New Rotterdammers and their visitors didn't generally approve of spending nights in health hazards.

Wrapper said, "I'm hungry."

. . . .

The Lincoln Hotel's narrow front was sandwiched between Seven Seas Tattoos and the Slingshot, a strip club. Directly across the street was a small diner with a large sign in its window claiming they had the biggest burgers in San Diego.

Scooter shouted "Bag Burkas," and dashed across Broadway. Wilson followed, then Halvard and, finally, Wrapper, who's shoelace had come untied.

They opened the diner's door and a tinny bell made a muffled sound. The bell had an old sock wrapped over it. In front of the serving bar, on one of five stools, sat a thick, unshaven man with unruly, black hair. No one else was in the place. On the wall behind the serving bar was painted naked maidens dancing around Greek columns.

Wrapper stared at the naked maidens and said dreamily, "Do you think they'll serve us beer?"

The thick, unshaven man swiveled on his stool to face them. He wore a Midas Muffler shirt that had "Achilles" stitched over a breast pocket. "Welcome," he said. "We are sailor country. You want beers?"

Wilson said, "Four. Make them Buds, long neck."

Achilles danced away gracefully, a Zorba of San Diego. When he came back with the beers and reached across Halvard, Halvard noted the stink of onions doused with an aftershave that should be banned. To Halvard, the odor was a reminder of lutefisk, the ritual food that all Norwegians had to face at least once in their lives. Did Greeks have a version of lutefisk? Halvard thought that when he saw the world, he'd make it a point, in every country he visited, to discover their most famous, worst food. Foods worse than lutefisk.

Achilles spoke as he wrote on his pad. "Four cheeseburgers fries. Coming soon. Like ship on time." He flowed back behind the grill, then stood beneath a photo of the Parthenon, flipping burgers with one hand while wiping sweat from his brow with the other. When his sweat hit the grill, it sizzled.

Wilson said. "We've got lot of places like this back home."

Scooter responded with, "Chiz Burkas."

Wrapper looked at Halvard and asked, "Where'd you say you're from?"

"New Rotterdam," Halvard said, adding the automatic tagline that every New Rotterdammer learns to do early in life. "It's an hour from Seattle."

"Hey, the Mariner's," said Wilson. "Griffey, Edgar, the Big Unit."

Scooter grew animated. "Grit pliers." He made a faux-swing with his hands, intending to hit one out of the park, but knocked over his beer instead. He saved it with quick hands.

"Nice catch," Wilson said. Wilson told them he played baseball in high school. He'd pitched some but was better at hitting.

Wrapper told them that the first time he got bare tit was under the baseball bleachers in high school.

Halvard had seen lots of baseball at New Rotterdam's Smelt Field, but never played.

Halvard said to Wrapper, "Minnesota, huh?"

"Yeah, Land of a Thousand Lakes, that's me."

"What do you do in Minnesota?"

"You know, stuff everyone does. Drink beer. Ice fish."

Halvard had never heard of ice fishing. The only fishing he ever did was off the banks of the Washcon River in the summer with his father. And the only drinking he'd ever done was at the Norwegian Cultural Center when his father would sneak him a few shots of Vikingfjord vodka, saying with a wink that they needed it if they were going to survive Mrs. Johannsen's herring hash.

Wilson said he was a Bud man all the way. Wrapper said that even though he was a Minnesotan, he preferred Coors, Regular Coors being better than Coors Lite. Halvard told them his hometown beer was Bernie's, though he'd never had one. Scooter liked "Bama Burr."

Wrapper said ice fishing was the best. "When everything's all iced up, you drive your truck or whatever out into the middle of a lake. You set up a little hut, and sit there with buddies jigging a short-armed pole into a hole and drink beer." Wrapper said it wasn't about catching fish. It was about trying write your name in pee on the ice when you were drunk. Halvard laughed. He wondered how Berthe would like ice fishing and name peeing.

"I'll have to try that sometime," Halvard said. He clinked his longneck Bud with Wrapper's.

Achilles arrived with the burgers and fries, saying something only Scooter understood. They both laughed, and then laughed at each other laughing. It was a laughter competition out of control. Scooter won after Achilles looked worried at him and left.

They all dove into their burgers.

"Not damn bad," said Wilson, ordering another round of beers. Halvard was already feeling tipsy, but what the hell, he thought. If seeing the world means more beer, who am I to argue? The world is a big place, bigger than you can imagine when you haven't seen much of it.

Wilson was getting relaxed and was talking a lot, telling stories of his 'hood and how most of his friends got shot. "That's why I had to book," he said. "The Navy ain't about guns."

Halvard wondered if Wilson, a black guy, felt weird about being around white guys. Like, was he pissed off that his great-great-great grandfather had to suffer slavery? Some people carry a grudge, Halvard knew, because his Uncle Einar blamed "Huns" for pretty much everything.

But he didn't know how to ask Wilson such a personal question, so he kept quiet. Keeping quiet was a good strategy. It had always worked for him. It worked at home, at school, and it worked with Berthe. As his mother constantly advised, always in a cheery voice, "It's better to be thought a fool than to open your mouth and remove all doubt."

Still, he figured a black man from Detroit and a white guy from Alabama were supposed to hate each other. It was like the Yankees and the Red Sox, or the Smelt and the Las Vegas Showstoppers. Both teams and their fans hated the other, even though they were both basically the same. Race conflict was a difficult thing to square. No one cared about race in New Rotterdam. Race was just an accident of birth, like being Norwegian.

"Nobody's born bad," Halvard's father told him. "We're all made in God's image." Halvard said that once to Berthe, and Berthe howled. She said if Mr. Rudy, the Wood Academy's custodian, was made in the image of God, then God's nose must be a real beauty. She told that story later at table during a St. Olaf's event for the homeless, and no one laughed. Berthe had great sardine sandwiches, but she couldn't always read an audience.

After a third round of beers were downed, Wrapper asked "What do we do now?"

"We go there," Wilson said, pointing out the window. Everyone turned and looked.

"To the Slingshot? "Wrapper said. "Cool."

"No, that's for later," said Wilson. "We want to go to the other side."

They all waved magnanimously to Achilles as if they'd see him again real soon and left the diner. Halvard left a two quarter tip on the table. Scooter, last to leave, picked it up while no one was looking.

When he was in the fourth grade, Halvard and his mother walked by Asbury's Tattoo on North New Rotterdam Avenue, across from the Old City Hall. When little Halvard stopped to look at Ashbury's window display, his mother grabbed him by the ear and dragged him away. That's all Halvard knew about tattoos. Of course, his mother wasn't here now, she'd been replaced by Wilson.

Wilson led his brood into Seven Seas Tattoos. The rest did their best to affect Wilson's worldly saunter, but with varying success. Wrapper got it best, Halvard a bit less, and Scooter wasn't even close.

"Slaw done," Scooter shouted, jogging to catch up.

Once inside the tattoo parlor, Wrapper found a three-ring binder that was crammed with examples of tattoos. They were drawn on paper behind plastic display sheets. Every type of mermaid imaginable came swimming forward, some drinking from bottles, one being languid beneath a palm tree, another smoking a joint as big as her leg. And anchors galore, a few with banners into which you could ink someone's name. Little red imps were popular, winking or wide-eyed. There was a Wile E. Coyote with an Acme anvil sunk into his head. The range of tattoo art is big, thought Halvard. As big as the world.

One little tattoo that caught his eye beckoned him like it was singing him onto the rocks. He didn't tell the others, but if he was going to get a tattoo, that was the one he'd get.

The Seven Seas tattooist was busy filling in the outline of a red devil on a customer's arm. The customer appeared to be as young as Halvard and Wrapper. He was lying prone in what appeared to be a dentist's chair.

The customer said, "Any one of you guys got a bullet? If you do, I'd bite it right now." He grimaced while forcing a smile, grasping both the tattoo chair's arms like they were the only thing between him and damnation.

"Doze eat pine yuz match?" asked Scooter.

The customer moaned.

"Be with you guys in a minute," said the tattooist. "Almost done here."

"Praise Jesus," the customer cried.

Wrapper held up the three-ring binder. "Ok, boys, who's in?"

. . . .

Dawn came early at the Lincoln Hotel. Halvard swung his legs over the side of his cot. He had been dreaming that he was in the Washcon State Corrections Facility just outside of New Rotterdam. He was an inmate and the jailer kept locking him in and out of different cells. The jailor was Berthe.

Wilson and Scooter were standing at the mirror examining their chessman knight tattoos. Wilson flexed his chessman and it seemed to rise on its hind legs. It was ready for battle. Scooter's chessman was wrapped around his skinny arm so couldn't be seen in its entirety from any angle.

"You'll grow into it," Wilson said. Scooter didn't look convinced.

"Luke's wired," Scooter said.

Wrapper was still in his cot wheezing in deep REM. His arm was draped over his head, his tattoo looking upward. It was a mermaid with kelp around her private parts.

Halvard wasn't entirely sure how the evening ended, though he remembered placing a folded dollar on the front of the stage where a rather beat up woman bumped but didn't grind. He remembered the softness of a boa floating across his face.

He kicked Wrapper's cot with his foot.

"I'm up," Wrapper said, pulling his sheet over his head.

"We're late," Wilson said, illustrating his leadership capacity by being the only one with a watch.

"We've got ten minutes to be out front," he said, grabbing his gear and walking to the door across brick-colored carpets that had seen their best days at least one grandma ago.

"I'm out," shouted Halvard, followed by Scooter, who yelled, "Ahm ought tow." Wrapper who was still buckling his belt, shoes untied, followed the others by hopping down the hallway on one leg while struggling to put on a shoe.

The foursome went down the stairs, past Chuck.

"Good luck, boys."

"Thanks, Chuck," they said in unison.

"Asshole," said a voice.

. . . .

The Naval Recruitment Center office was just three blocks away. To Halvard, it looked like any storefront at the South Washcon Mall. The office space next door was vacant. A piece of cardboard covered the corner of one of its broken windows.

A line was forming outside the office, perhaps fifty or sixty young fellows, no women. Halvard was surprised there were no women. Wilson was disappointed.

"No tang," he said, standing at the end of the line. The others followed lined up behind him.

Seconds later, the front door opened and out walked a sailor who looked as if he'd been sent by central casting. Hollywood handsome, with leading man looks, a resplendent gold braid dangled from his shoulder. He looked enticingly worldly. The braid of gold caressed red chevrons. He looked like a hero who didn't walk, but strutted, knowing how good he looked. His white sailor's cap was slightly cocked to the side. His uniform was creaseless, the belled flare of his trousers perfectly tailored. He wore highly polished, gleaming black shoes. He was one of those men whose smile revealed nothing but its own beauty. Brad Pitt would be jealous of him.

Behind Brad Pitt's look-alike was a Marine who looked more like a hit-man than a Hollywood actor. "Two lines," he shouted. "Marines on the left, sailors on the right." "Not that left, dipwad," the Marine shouted, pointing at some unlucky bastard. "The other one." His psychological profile was no doubt the subject of many informal discussions.

Halvard and Wrapper looked to Wilson. Each prayed Wilson would never leave their side.

Once he was in the sailor line, Halvard observed that Marine recruits looked no different than sailor recruits. He expected Marines would be bigger and more athletic than sailors, but it wasn't true. While there were some big bruisers in both lines, most were just skinny kids like him and Wrapper. Few of them were older. One Marine had a huge booger dangling from his left nostril. To Halvard, he looked like he could have been Scooter's smarter cousin.

Halvard further noticed that at least half of the guys in both lines were black. New Rotterdam's black population was pretty small, certainly much smaller than were Asians or Lutherans. Racism was virtually non-existent in New Rotterdam. When a black family decided to call New Rotterdam home, New Rotterdammers treated them like visiting royalty. At least they did at St. Olaf's.

Before they were all told to shut up and stand at attention, Wilson busied himself by greeting other black guys as if they were old family members at a reunion. Like members of a private club, they shared an elaborate handshake. The Sons of Olaf, of which Halvard's father was a lifelong member, had a special handshake too. But the Sons of Olaf handshake was a piker compared to the black guys at the Naval Recruitment Center. Sons of Olaf handshakes didn't actually involve the hands, only the fingers. It was really more of a finger shake, two fingers of one right hand grasped by two fingers of another right hand, after which both parties would say, "Olaf Ser Dig." (Olaf Sees You.)

As far as Halvard could tell, blacks gripped hands like they were getting ready to arm wrestle. Their hands grappled, all parts of the hand involved. Once the entire hand had been grasped then loosed, both hands flew up and then flew down, the ritual ending with a light chest bump as athletes do before they beat each other's brains out on the field of play.

Wilson said to one future sailor, "You know it, bro." Halvard felt "Olaf Ser Dig" sounded more sincere.

Everything moved quickly after that. The Marine that had the worrisome psychological profile shouted someone's name and someone shouted back, "Here."

The Marine stopped, took a deep breath like someone had just seriously disappointed him, and shouted louder, "That's here, sir, maggot."

The recruit shouted back, "Here, sir, maggot."

Someone else laughed. Big mistake. The Marine with psychological issues was not a fan of laughter. He shouted, "Ok, smart ass. Lesson number one. One person fucks up, everyone pays. If you don't like it, don't let anyone fuck up. How hard is that? I'll let you think about it for ten seconds." Three seconds later he shouted, "Everyone hit the deck. Give me ten."

All the black guys to a man hit the deck and started doing pushups. Most of the white guys followed, but two of the younger white guys looked confused and kept standing. One was the one who had a booger dangling from his nostril.

The psychological basket case in charge shouted, "You pasty-faced ass-packers stand there like something wrong with you." He waited for a moment, then asked, "Well, is there something wrong with you?"

No one uttered a sound. He walked over to the two young white guys and clamped a meaty hand on each of their shoulders and squeezed them to the ground. Halvard thought the booger guy was going to cry.

"Ok, ladies, now give me twenty," the Marine ordered. Halvard felt relief for the booger guy who held himself together. "No, better make it twenty-five. You wanted the Marines and now you got the Marines."

Standing next to Halvard, Wrapper said in a hushed voiced, "Jesus H. Christ."

Halvard nodded his agreement. If one wanted to serve their country or escape the law or just plain find something better to do than waste their time at home, or, like Halvard, see the world, the Marines were not the way to go.

Once all the Marines said, "Here, sir," correctly, they were boarded onto yellow school buses parked on the street in front of the Recruitment Center. The psychotic terrorist in charge went with them, leaving Brad Pitt with his cocked snow-white cap, gold braid, and red stripes and slash marks on his sleeve standing in front of the sailors.

He strode around to face his line of recruits. "Glad you didn't join the Marines?" he said. His smile was warm and wicked, a smile Brad Pitt would adopt when he wasn't supposed to be trusted.

Brad Pitt began to read names, asking the recruits to simply say, "here, sir." It seemed almost a genteel request, compared to what just happened to the Marines. Of course, everyone already knew not to add any words to that statement, especially not "maggot."

Wilson bellowed, "Here, sir" in a strong voice after Brad called, "Wilson." Halvard, Scooter, and Wrapper nodded to each other as if Wilson had just done something extraordinary.

Wrapper sang, "Here, sir" after hearing Brad Pitt call out "Thump." That was Wrapper's real name? Wrapper Thump? Scooter grinned widely, revealing all his remaining teeth.

Halvard answered "Here, sir" when his last name was called and Wrapper backslapped him on the sly. Scooter giggled, then made a sound not unlike one a small animal makes when chewing its food.

Brad Pitt said, "I don't know how to pronounce this one, but I'll try....Mistletwerp."

Scooter shouted back, "Haw, saw."

After everyone had been accounted for, as had happened to the Marines, they were led to two yellow school busses. Wilson and Scooter and Wrapper were directed to one yellow bus and hopped on. Halvard was made to hop on the other one.

Halvard wasn't to see his new pals again. Tattoos disappearing in the mists of time. So goes the world.

. . . .

In front of Boot Camp's high-wired gates, Halvard and his new group, about thirty of them, were told to stand in line. They did not yet know it, but the most fundamental of all naval activities is standing in line. Their introduction to line standing involved facing a six-lane thoroughfare while standing at rigid attention. Across the street was a billboard featuring a bikini-clad girl selling Toyotas.

Brad Pitt said, "Keep your eyes on her, boys. Don't let me see you not looking at her." Then he left. Halvard kept staring at the girl in the bikini. It was red and skimpy. She pooched her tan butt at every passing car, several of which had passengers that leaned from their windows to yell insults at Halvard and his fellow recruits.

After an hour of standing in line facing the billboard, Brad Pitt showed up again. He said his name was Mr. Hayworth, a First Class Boatswain's Mate. "That's pronounced Bosun, not Boat's Swain," he said. "Don't forget that. You get that wrong and…" His veiled threat hung in the air like a noose. Soon after Mr. Hayworth's return, they were marched to the infirmary for a mandatory checklist physical.

"You have any complaints?" an older sailor wearing a white coat asked. His eyes were terribly bloodshot and he smelled of bleach.

"No," Halvard said.

"No?" the guy repeated, letting the question mark hang in the air above them like some mysterious guiding star. Halvard easily deduced his error.

"No, sir," he said, snapping to attention even though he was already at attention.

"Good," the guy said, clearly not meaning it. "Next."

Then they went to the barber shop, a small room made of concrete blocks that smelled of burnt rubber. His haircut took less than 15 seconds. Zip zip. When Halvard caught his reflection in a window, he thought he looked like a hairless cat. Thirty hairless cats were then ushered through another door where Mr. Hayworth was waiting. He told them to stand in a line that would go nowhere for another hour. Before leaving he told them they were assigned to Company 661 and not to forget it.

"If you want to see the world, stand in line" may not be a good motto, but it was an important truth. Halvard took line standing seriously. He rose to his full height, squared his shoulders back and went into what Berthe called, "The Halvard Zone." Eyes straight ahead, brain on autopilot, standing as rigid as they come. Unfortunately, he kept nodding, and heard Mr. Hayworth shout, "What's with all the nodding, squirrel? Are you a yo-yo?" Halvard made his neck rigid instantly. Nodding worked in New Rotterdam, but probably not in the world.

Next, Halvard and the others were stripped of their civilian clothes, or civvies, as Boot Camp lingo had it. They all shoved their civvies into canvas sacks before tossing those into larger sacks, and then into even larger sacks that took three men to lift. He never saw his civvies again, though he was given someone else's civvies when he left boot camp. As far as he knew his civvies were distributed to needy customers at the Lincoln Hotel.

After his civvies were taken from him, Halvard was issued a pair of black dress shoes, a pair of black boots, two pairs of black socks that came in a plastic sleeve. He was given two boxer shorts and white t-shirts, then two sets of new, stiff dungarees, two light blue shirts, a darker blue jacket, and a ball cap. None of his new clothes fit, except for the ball cap. Fat guys couldn't get their pants to button and skinny guys looked like they sported denim moo moos.

Mr. Hayworth then marched his recruits to a series of old wooden buildings, where Mr. Hayworth stopped in front of one of them. "Okay, squirrels, take a good look," he said. Halvard, quick to catch on, noted that being a squirrel was a bad thing. Mr. Hayworth said, "This is your home for the next three months. Don't forget it, cause should you forget where you live you'll be fucking with me. And you don't want to fuck with me. You might as well fuck your mother." He let that sink in. "You wouldn't fuck your mother, would you?"

Everyone agreed that it would not be a good idea to fuck their mother or Mr. Hayworth, but they didn't say so aloud. Speaking out loud was not a preferred skill as was standing in line. Rather, they acceded to Mr. Hayworth's worldview by being shit scared. The Lincoln Hotel was Eden compared to Boot Camp. Boot Camp was more like being with Berthe. But Berthe wasn't there, and Boot Camp would end after thirteen weeks. God punishes man so that he will appreciate whatever good might happen later. After thirteen weeks, Halvard, Berthe free, would be able to see the world in earnest. Thank you, God.

Company 661 spent most of those thirteen weeks cleaning the barracks, though not without drama. One guy wet his bed and another didn't like to shower. Both soon disappeared. One morning, after Mr. Hayworth had awakened everyone by throwing a metal trash can along the floor the length of the barracks, he introduced his assistant, Mr. Culpepper. Mr. Hayworth, like all other Company Commanders, needed an assistant because otherwise he couldn't drink beer all day at the Enlisted Men's Club.

Mr. Culpepper, Mr. Hayworth explained, had recently graduated from Boot Camp. Mr. Hayworth said anyone might be so honored if they proved to be a "top dog." Halvard thought briefly that he might want to be a top dog, but concluded that survival was more important, so he kept his mouth shut.

Halvard decided Mr. Culpepper was in training to become a sociopath with a squirrel fetish. His favorite saying was, "I wouldn't feed you old corn."

. . . .

Halvard's bunk was one of a row of bunks separated only by a metal locker. Each recruit shared his bunk with a bunkmate. One topside, one down below. Halvard's bunkmate was from Alabama. He was topside and Halvard was below. Halvard didn't understand him any more than he'd understood Scooter. No one else understood him either, and someone gave him the nickname, "Fuck Stick."

"Don't suppose you know a guy named Scooter?" Halvard asked Fuck Stick. Fuck Stick's reply was a moan with two k's. Halvard immediately missed Wilson. Seeing the world without a translator was tough duty.

For the next few weeks, Company 661 marched, went to bed at 9pm, got up at 5am and marched again. They marched in straight lines, in circles. They learned to pivot smartly and not be "loser squirrels." Skill development in all the important areas of Navy life apparently required much marching.

Marching was suspended only for one thing during these first weeks. That was chow hall. Boot Camp must have gotten a deal on potatoes, because that was the basis of Chow Hall cuisine. Potatoes and mystery meat. Halvard, who had never weighed more than

130 pounds, put on fifteen pounds during his thirteen weeks. Was weight gain a Navy skill?

At chow hall, Company 661 first lined up next to the dumpsters. That way, it was easier for the seagulls to shit on recruits before they ate. Seagull management was another Navy skill requirement, the skill being don't get shit on if you can help it.

Hundreds of seagulls circled above Boot Camp's dumpsters. Barracks chatter had it that seagulls ought to be called shit-gulls or squirrel-gulls. Flying rats, Halvard's father called them. Whenever a recruit got shat on by a seagull, he had to double time it back to the barracks with a buddy, change into his other shirt, then double time it back. Halvard, luckily, was always a gull shit-buddy, not a victim. Double timing it back to the barracks and waiting for the shat-on to change shirts was a welcome break, providing Halvard with time to be alone with his thoughts.

Some guys wrote letters home, Halvard didn't. He figured he had better things to do like learn how to smoke. He and others smoked cigarettes under the barracks porch when it was windy. Obviously, Navy recruits had been smoking under the barracks porch during windstorms for a very long time. Halvard found graffiti claiming, "Bozo Was Here, 1968," "Shirley Blew Me Before I Left," written in 1975, and "Woe is Me," dated 1952.

Halfway through Boot Camp, marching became interspersed with actual education. The Navy's pedagogy was simple: half the squirrels will learn to go port and the other half will learn to go starboard. The Navy didn't want its squirrels running into each other during emergencies such as sinking. Halvard also took a battery of tests designed to discover what kind of sailor the Navy would decide he should be. Halvard thought he might like to become a bosun's mate like Mr. Hayworth. That would be a great way to see the world. Out in the open air with your shirt off, wowing Polynesian girls. Maybe by then he'd have an armful of tattoos, telling his own stories of adventure.

Unfortunately, Halvard turned out not to be bosun mate material, but office worker material. Halvard's failure in this regard was because he was a virtuoso typist.

It was his mother's fault. She insisted he take typing class in high school, saying "learn something for God's sake." His father added, "I don't care what he does, so long as it's legal." Halvard took typing class in high school because the classroom was filled with girls other than Berthe.

It was during their last weeks of Boot Camp when Mr. Hayworth passed out the test results. He said, "There'll be a list of three ratings. You get to choose one, though that doesn't mean much. The Navy knows best. They'll send you where you can do the most good." He stopped and smiled. "Or the least bad, depending."

Halvard raised his hand for the first time in thirteen weeks, having kept his trap shut from the moment he laid eyes on the bikini selling Toyotas. Mr. Hayworth acknowledged Halvard by pointing at him, and Halvard said, "On mine, Mr. Hayworth, sir, down at the bottom, it says, 'A School, San Diego.'"

"That means you've been selected to go for further training. To what the Navy calls, "A School."

"A school?"

"No, not a school," Mr. Hayworth said. "A School. There's also a B School and a C School, but don't worry about that. Here, give me your papers." Halvard marched to Mr. Hayworth, gave him the papers, spun on his heels and marched back to where he'd been.

"In your case, you'll be going to Yeoman "A" School…where you'll learn how to type and file in ways the Navy likes," Mr. Hayworth said. Then he snickered, "…but most importantly, how the old man likes his coffee."

Boot Camp and Yeoman A School were separated by a barbed wire fence, world's apart. In A School no one was called squirrel, and there were no bunkbeds, but single beds, more comfortable than Boot Camp's mattresses of torture. The barracks was a block of concrete, newly built. Halvard decided to consider A School a type of promotion. He remembered when his father became gang boss, he called it "going in the right direction." Halvard felt he was going in the right direction, too, unconsciously nodding in honor of his father.

The biggest skill Halvard learned in A School was remembering which form had to be filled out so that nothing would (a) sink into the sea, or (b) get you thrown into the brig. Those forms were also required to be filled out and filed within certain time restrictions. He'd never had to remember as much information in such a short amount of time since his father showed him how to use a riding mower.

Halvard's strategy for achievement was to remember just enough to pass the tests, then instantly forget what he'd learned.

After all, it was the same strategy he'd employed in high school, and that had worked well enough to get him into the Navy. Hell, it was how he got through most of his conversations with Berthe.

After graduating from A School, fourth from the bottom of his class, Halvard was ready to see the world. He felt at the helm of his life. The captain of his own ship, the USS Halvard. The wide, wide world was beckoning to him and he was eager to follow it.

Then his orders came. Whatever their reason, the Navy instructed him to get his orders from a postal clerk. The postal clerk handed Halvard a brown manila envelope. "Where you wanting to go?" the clerk asked.

"Anyplace except where I'm from," Halvard said. "Asia, Mideast, Northern Europe, Mediterranean, doesn't matter to me. Just want to see the world, that's all."

Tearing at the brown manila envelope, Halvard read the document before reaching the door. It was indecipherable. The document seemed to have been generated by a computer that only spoke to other computers. Reading it was like trying to understand Scooter. Everything was in code. Where was Wilson?

Halvard turned and went back to stand in line, waiting for the postal clerk.

"Pardon me," Halvard said to the clerk when it was his turn.

"Hey man, back so soon? What's up?"

"Actually, I don't know, I can't read these orders. It's like gibberish."

"That's because it is gibberish. Navy gibberish. Lucky for you, I speak Navy gibberish." The postal clerk laughed. "Here, hand it over, let me give it a try."

Halvard handed his orders to the clerk, excited to hear where in the world he was going. The Navy sailed all around the world. Who knew where he'd end up? It could be anywhere. Halvard felt himself on the edge of a brand new way of being. He was ready. Ready to see the world.

The postal clerk scanned the document briefly and grinned. "Son, you are one freaking lucky guy."

"Really?" Halvard said, imagining himself in Marseille with Tom Cruise again. His hair would be flying in the ocean breeze as he sailed from one port to another. He took a deep breath and began nodding. He hadn't been so excited to see the world since his father signed his enlistment papers.

"Deliver me into the wide, wide world, O God," he thought. "Beyond Berthe. Beyond New Rotterdam."

"Where, where?" Halvard pled.

"Killer duty."

"Where, man? Where in the world am I going?"

The clerk paused. It was like he was waiting for an imaginary drum roll to finish. He leaned forward for emphasis, "You're going to the freakin' Space Needle, dude."

"What? Huh?"

"You lucky bitch. You've been assigned to the Seattle Naval Recruiting Center."

. . . .

"Halvard, is that a tattoo?" Berthe asked. Around them were several tables filled with fabulous plates of Lutheran foods. Berthe had brought five plates of her famous sardine sandwiches, and had placed one before Halvard at their table for two. She would eat them all. She wore an extra comfy peasant blouse and generous skirt. She looked like a girl Achilles the Greek might hustle if he were a Lutheran.

It was Veterans Day, five months after Halvard had first reported for duty at the Seattle Recruiting office.

It was his day off and he dutifully drove the hour from Seattle to New Rotterdam in order to please his mother. She told him Marjorie Veck and Hattie Vanderhuek, sole members of St. Olaf's

Veterans Committee were holding a Pickle Ball Tournament. Halvard's mother had run into them at Washcon Grocery.

"It's to honor our veterans, all of them, including your son," Marjorie said. Hattie added, "And we're selling baked goods for charity."

Berthe wanted Halvard be her doubles partner. His mother said, "She's looking forward to it, so put on a good face."

And now he was here, at a table for two with Berthe who had just seen the outline of his tattoo. He leaned forward and stretched his arms out. The fabric of his short sleeved shirt rose up. He hadn't shown anyone in New Rotterdam until then.

"It is a tattoo," Berthe said admiringly, as if it were a dessert.

Halvard began to nod.

"What is it?" Berthe asked? She prayed to St. Olaf that it be a tattoo of her name. She looked at Halvard with maternal fondness. She put her hand on his.

Halvard, nodding like a metronome, pulled the sleeve up, revealing the entirely of his tattoo.

"It's the world," he said.

Berthe was disappointed. "A globe? You got a tattoo of a globe? Why a globe?"

"I wanted to see the world and now I always will."

An ancient, respected Navy skill is the telling of sea stories. Halvard wasn't skilled at telling sea stories yet. He was still in the stage known as outright lying.

He looked at Berthe, stopped nodding for a moment, and said. "I got it for you."

Berthe's disappointment over the tattoo melted away in an instant. "Oh, Halvard. Thank you. Thank you," she said. "I'd love to see the world with you." She rose from her chair and looked at him with narrowed eyes, "But right now I need pie."

Hong's Moral

If you and I met in a neighborhood bar, you'd find me a most charming fellow. And charm matters in the real world. Charming others is how people get things done. My mother told me that. She said, "Charm suggests confidence, and people are drawn to confident persons." It doesn't matter if you are hawking trinkets from the trunk of your car, or trying to get a moron elected to high position, you need top notch people skills. As good old mom said to me on the night of my high school graduation, "Honey, you were born with charm. Don't waste it."

Eight years later, having taken my gift of charm into the real world, I hit a serious snag. My charm offensive was barely paying my bar bill. Part of my problem was that in addition to charm, I had developed a lousy attitude. The only job I could find supporting a lousy attitude was as a night security patrolman walking around a gated car dealership. I carried a radio and a flashlight, one of which generally worked.

Thanks, mom. You should have been a football coach instructing your players to practice by running into brick walls.

I needed a change. A change of place, a change of job. But where to go? What to do? I discussed it with an ad hoc group of barflies, and shortly before closing we decided I should go to Thailand, if only to "check things out." Over the next days I gathered up what meager savings I had and turned my back on my career as a security man.

I calculated I could survive in Thailand for at least three months, maybe four months if I was careful, which I rarely was. My plane ticket and passport in hand, off I flew, chasing my carelessness down the rabbit hole of life, into the unknown with no expectations other than to survive by doing something different in a different place than where I was.

I decided Chiang Mai was the place for me, and after arriving, I found cheap lodgings. It was a shack behind a house with seven children, all of whom should have been in diapers, but weren't. I stowed my clothes and toiletries in the cardboard box that served as a closet and I went out to find a low rent bar. Why? Primarily, because that's where the beer is. But of equal importance to me was that beer attracts barflies, and barflies are always willing to chat with a new guy in town.

I found a suitable dive within walking distance, drawn into it by its metal roof and bamboo slats instead of curtains. I like places that look about ready to fall down. It gives them a certain societal edginess I find encouraging. The bar was a folding table top sitting atop wooden pallets, fronted by rattan barstools that had seen better days. I sat on one, ordering a Singha beer from the twelve year old bartender.

There was a man sitting on a neighboring stool. He seemed sane enough, so I introduced myself. He said his name was Ambrose Berg.

Berg was as charming as I once thought myself to be, and his attitude was anything but lousy. Instantly my spirits improved.

We spent that afternoon talking about Chiang Mai, life in general, and traded biographical bits and pieces of ourselves. The beer flowed freely and we quickly developed a camaraderie. No wonder they invented the term, "Happy Hour." My first day in town, and already I'd met a friend. Things were already looking up. By the end of my second week in Chiang Mai, Berg and I were meeting daily.

Berg was masculine in the very best way. Not only was he self-assured, he was also self-deprecating, acutely funny, a keen observer of the human comedy. He clearly enjoyed being himself and, as every sot knows, men of good natured vanity make the most stimulating drinking pals.

We discovered we shared an ignorance of practical skills. Neither or us could saw or hammer, garden or weld. Computers were a bore. We decided we were good with braggadocio and white lies, but you wouldn't want to ask us to fix something that was broken. In fact, we believed practical skills were essentially a liability. A waste of time. Time that could be better put to use in the service of bullshitting.

"Bullshit refreshes the world," Berg said, adjusting the magenta strap of his Apple Watch Hermes. "It's a basic need of man. I don't know why Maslow didn't include it on his list."

I said, "If you didn't listen to bullshitters, how would you know which politicians to hate?" He laughed. The naturalness of his guffaw was unaffected and hardy.

A decade apart in age, Berg being the elder, he knew a lot about philosophy and drinking. I knew a lot about drinking. He said we were the type of men who grabbed life with both hands, "unless, of course, one of those hands is holding a beer." His company was compelling, filled with subtle hilarity. Often, when later remembering something he said, I'd chuckle. On the big screen we could have played small town conmen buddies. Berg, the brains, me his straight man.

Berg said he was from the "shadows of Seattle." I told him I was originally from Radnor, Ohio, but we moved to Portland when I was four, so I have no memory of Radnor, Ohio. I said perhaps my mother made the whole thing up. "Say it like it's true, even if it isn't" was one of her favorite lines.

Berg clapped when he heard this. "She sounds like she has Utilitarian tendencies," he said.

"I don't know about that," I said. "But she is Catholic."

Berg's father was a mover and shaker in his hometown, New Rotterdam. My father, who I hadn't seen in many years, was a man who got moved and shook.

Berg said he was "wealthy-ish" and by his manner of dress, I concluded he wasn't lying. He always wore a linen jacket over an expensive t-shirt, matching them with Tommy Bahama shorts and Mexican leather sandals. He said he lived for a time in Mexico before moving to Thailand, a time he said he spent exploring his "inner Malcolm Lowry." His attitude was that of a man amused by his money.

I wore faded Levi cutoffs, accessorizing them with flip flops and a torn Nirvana t-shirt.

. . . .

Berg had a calligraphy teacher, Master Hong. I knew nothing of calligraphy, and when Berg suggested I join him for a few sessions with Hong I eagerly agreed. Berg had been picking up the tab whenever we were together and I was beginning to think I might be able squeeze a couple more months out of Thailand. If survival required me to take calligraphy lessons, so be it.

Berg arrived at my place in a Tuk Tuk. The Tuk Tuk took us us to Hong's place, a shack. Not quite a shack, actually. More like how Frank Gehry might design a cardboard box. It featured a dusty patio facing the street. Around a small round patio table was seating for three. The table was thickly built, its base made of elephant hoof (my guess) or a type of exotic, nearly extinct hard wood (Berg's).

We sat facing cars and motorbikes as they competed with bicycles for the right of way. Urban debris swirled around our feet like minuscule tornados. I heard a sound behind me and turned my head to see what it was. It was a man wearing worse flip flops than mine. They clapped as he walked. It was Hong.

"Berg," Hong howled, taking the seat between us.

"Berg friend to me," Hong said, reaching to touch my hand. I noticed he had two fingers missing. He wore a patch over one eye. My immediate judgment was that Hong looked like a beaten man. I had no idea if life had been kind or cruel to Hong, but either way it had left him worse for wear. But that was only my first impression. Soon enough I came to know the real Hong, as he was drunk on his ass within the hour.

Hong was a terrible drunk, not mean, but not funny or witty either. He was more of the blithering type, one you could barely understand when sober, let alone after a several quarts of Singha beer. Drunk, he sounded like a barfly in Star Wars.

We met Hong at 10am, as Berg and I agreed mid-morning was a civilized time to have one's first beer. Our metal chairs were rusty, topped by silk pillows that had seen better days. I know nothing of seat cushions except the one my mother bought when I was young.

She got it from a thrift shop. It was old and worn, patched with the remnant of a tablecloth featuring the fragment of a pumpkin. Though it was secondhand and threadbare, I loved that cushion. I carried it everywhere. I cuddled it so much it eventually began stinking of every foul smell my small hands could lay on it. And even it smelled better than Hong's silk pillows. I think the pillow I sat on originally belonged to Hong's dog, a cur with unrelenting mange who constantly stared at me like I was its last hope.

"Hong's a gas, don't you think?" Berg said to me while Hong unfurled the ratty bed sheet that kept his calligraphy tools.

"I like people who aren't afraid to be themselves," I said. "Agreed. Agreed," said Berg, clapping me on the shoulder.

Hong's calligraphic technique was translated to me by Berg as meaning "Tree Drunk Soldier Hand," of which Hong was a reputed master. From what I could see, Master Hong's mastery was limited to spilling ink and beer.

Hong's pedagogy was to write poems in Tree Drunk Soldier Hand, then ask us to decipher them. They looked like Rorschach blots.

"Is it about elephant sex?" I asked when presented one sheet of blots.

"No," Hong said, bluntly, followed by something undecipherable.

Berg translated. "He says you lack Buddha spirit."

Perhaps, I thought, but that's no reason to be rude. Didn't he know you shouldn't act like an idea snob while you have spittle on your chin? I assessed Hong more sharply after that.

Hong owned two dingy t-shirts, one with stains and the other with more stains. He paired these with khaki, knee-length Bermudas that revealed legs the same size as his arms, the diameter and tautness of a large rice noodle. His bald head was the shape of a large gourd, the back of it tapered as if it had been extruded from his exceptional forehead. Hong could have sold his forehead for advertising space.

Hong's constant smile was toothy and toothless at the same time, as it featured a single fang. The fang rose from the dark bottom of his goofy smile like an insulting middle finger. He must have brushed it with garlic. Locals referred to him by spitting a vowel out of their lower throat.

The three of us met twice again that week, the blot guessing sessions interrupted by lunch, always crispy garlic roll, curry puffs, and dancing shrimp. A small boy delivered it in a wooden box as big as his back. By the end of lunch Hong was generally so drunk that he invariably began to shout Thai profanities and shadow box imaginary figures.

"Perhaps he's doing battle with the ghosts of his ancestors," I quipped while Hong stroke his ink-stained chin braid, his face's premier adornment.

"My bet is mental disease," Berg said.

Of course being entertained by a mumbling sot has its limitations. After six sessions with Hong we parted company with him just as the Year of the Pig turned into the Year of the Rat. Berg immediately found another dive for us to meet in, one run by an ancient Thai woman with a soft spot in her heart for Americans. It is a rare feeling to be adored by your bartender, a feeling I recommended highly.

Hong did leave us with one life lesson. He wrote it down in Tree Drunk Soldier Hand. I still have it somewhere. Of course we couldn't decipher it and it took an hour of interrogating Hong to grasp what he was failing to transmit. Berg and I were quick studies when it came to communicating with drunken mimes. Mimes do their best work when drunk. Most people don't know that. At any rate, we eventually understood what Hong was saying. "Pretend to know what you are doing."

We called it Hong's Moral, though we could have just as easily named it after my mother.

....

It was my fourth month in Chiang Mai when I was forced to face the fact that my funds were running low. Even though Berg was buying all my drinks and, much of the time, my food, I knew my time in Thailand was coming to an end. Due to a lack of funds, I was beginning to panic. What the hell was I going to do when I got back to the USA? Find another security job?

With Berg I kept my mood jovial as I didn't want to bum him out. But Berg was an astute observer of other people's inner drama. He quickly figured me out. We were sitting outside a cafe. It was early, we hadn't had our third beer yet. I remember I'd been observing a dust devil dancing around a palm tree.

Berg said, "I've been thinking about you, what you're going to do next in your life."

"A tough subject," I said, warming up to self-pity.

"It doesn't need to be," Berg said. "In fact, I think I might have a solution."

"Really?" I said without enthusiasm.

Berg looked at me until I caught his eye. He said, "How'd you like to work for me?"

I was stunned into silence. I'm ashamed to admit it, but my first thought was that Berg made his money as a drug smuggler. After all, his fondness for linen did make him look like a featured player in Miami Vice.

I stammered, my mind scattered with wondering if I could make it being a drug mule.

Berg saw my discomfort. "Nothing weird," he said, waving his hand dismissively. "To be perfectly honest, your company over these past months truly has been excellent. A tonic, really. I can't remember my mood being so uplifted. Perhaps I feel I owe you something for that. Something in gratitude."

"You already pay for all my beer and dancing shrimp," I said.

"True," he said, standing to ponder the thought. He took a couple of steps away from me, then turned, pointing at me with his finger. "And that means you deserve a promotion."

"Promotion?"

"Yes, from being my beer peer to worthy assistant. As it happens, I'm in dire need of an assistant. It wouldn't be a hard job. You'd simply make decisions as I would make them. It'll be a snap for you. In case you haven't noticed, in just four months we've become like fraternal twins. Why stop now?"

I didn't think twice, or once, for that matter. I was living on fumes. I had no options, good or bad. My adventure in Thailand was coming to its natural end. I had to take Berg's offer. Even if things didn't work out, it would be a step up for me. Besides, Berg was correct, we did think alike. We shared the DNA of confidence men.

Before I could speak, Berg handed me a small box wrapped in white silk with a grey silk bow on top. Was Berg giving me Nordstrom cufflinks?

"Forgive me," Berg said," I presumed you'd accept my offer, so I had these made."

It was a box of 250 business cards. I picked one from the box and read it. Ambrose Berg Enterprises, LLC was printed across its top with my name in embossed letters beneath. And beneath my name was printed, "Executive Special Assistant."

"There is one issue, though I doubt a difficult one for a world traveler like you," Berg said. "You'll need to move."

"Move?"

"Yes. To New Rotterdam. That's where the job is."

I arrived in New Rotterdam three days later.

. . . .

Afternoon sunlight angled through the window blinds, waking me. I'd been napping in a Promenade Casual Leather Recliner, warmed by a red-green-gold Melody Johnson quilt. These were furnishings in the vast elegant apartment Berg had arranged for me. It was on the topmost floor of a remodeled warehouse known as Old Admin. When I left Chiang Mai, Berg told me "one cannot be a landlord unless one is first a lord. And no one can be a lord unless they have a penthouse."

Old Admin's eye-catching penthouse had been created by Washcon Design & Build, LLC, a division of Berg Real Estate Investors, LLC. As I looked upwards from my slumber, I let my eyes wander across old growth fir beams. They lent the space instant grandeur, massive wooden planks beautifully cured and cracked by nature, larger than Paul Bunyan's fingers.

The walls were original brick without insulation, requiring three large Finnish HVAC units to keep the studio toasty in winter, breezy in summer. I kept the temperature at a consistent seventy degrees. No matter how dismal New Rotterdam's gray weather, I could have been living in San Diego.

The ceiling was twelve feet high and the Finnish units hung from the fir beams like chandeliers. The kitchen's expensive stainless steel appliances were a brand I'd neither heard of nor remembered. Nearby was the bed, a white, round Luigi Massoni called a Lullaby Due. I came to refer to it as the Trampoline. In one corner of the room, near the half-wall, was a huge, handcrafted metal vase Washcon Design & Build, LLC had shipped in from Belgium. Sprouting from it was a rare Indonesian rubber plant. The floors were covered by ancient Persian rugs.

A spacious bathroom was installed with an infrared sauna and a power shower (four jets with dial choices ranging between Gentle Mist and Maximum Thrust). It was situated behind the half-wall faced by a Japanese mural. Sitting on the toilet, you were becalmed by seeing graceful cranes and monkeys climbing a tree.

Old Admin was once the administrative offices of New Rotterdam Grain & Malt, one of several brick buildings in a section of New Rotterdam called The Brewery. Other old brick buildings in the area, formerly the commercial center of the city, were slowly being gobbled up by New Rotterdam University. Near Old Admin were the new Music & Arts Building, formerly Washcon Cold Storage & Feed, and the university's Center for Craft Beer, an Art Deco structure that had once, ironically, housed Berg's cosmically wealthy father's earliest venture, Saul Berg Realty. The Berg name was on all manner of signs and plaques around the University. I remember briefly thinking I should change my last name to Berg, but then last call was announced and I forgot about it.

A group of Seattle lawyers had originally bought Old Admin after it had been vacant for a couple of decades. They promoted the project as "middle-income" housing, though only for permit and tax purposes, as their true intent was upscale condos. Halfway into the project, however, the lawyers fell out and began suing each other. Greed does not like to be upstaged by the greedier. The property was put up for sale. After sitting idle for a year, an expert in extracting value from distressed properties snapped it up.

That expert was Arnold Dimple, Senior VP of Berg Urban Investments, LLC. "Twenty cents on the dollar," Dimple bragged when I met him. Dimple said he had purchased Old Admin with Berg in mind. "I hoped Ambrose would come to his senses. Maybe get his commercial chops up to speed. Instead," he scowled, "he sent you."

Dimple handed me a credit card. It was for an account at the New Rotterdam National Bank. "I trust you'll spend wisely," he said. "But I'm not counting on that. If you work for Ambrose, you're probably not thrifty."

Dimple gave me the details of my job expectations. "Manage it," he said, taking a deep breath. "As best you can. And don't burn it down." He reached into his pocket and retrieved a business card. He handed it to me. It was Dimple's, on which he'd underlined his phone number. "And there's this." He handed me a small linen envelope. In it was a note from Berg.

"I have always dreamed of being artist," he wrote. "Alas, It is my fate to merely be a man who can buy anything he wants. This is the reason I hired you. For you to be the me I always wanted to be." He signed it with a smiley face.

Yes, my liege. Your wastefulness is my command.

If I were going to live as Berg, I figured I should do my best to mimic him. So I adopted his manner, his wardrobe, his style of hair. I began to ape his speech patterns, adopting his tendency to lower his face when looking at someone. Step by step, I found myself becoming Berg's emotional doppelgänger. Less me, more Berg.

I bought a magnificent stainless steel drawing table, a 72-inch wide screen TV, and dozens of books on art. If I was to manage artist's digs and be the artist my employer expected himself to be, I figured I should know something about art. There were bookcases in the penthouse made of polished cherry wood and I filled them with art books. It became a collection any small liberal arts college would murder donors for.

I arranged for the delivery of a little less than an acre of canvas that ended up either leaning against the studio's walls, pre-stretched or remaining in their rolls of plastic, stacked in a corner like alien cocoons. Then I ordered a truckload of paints and brushes from New Rotterdam Art Supply, enough to paint a bridge.

I stacked roughly one hundred books on the floor next to the English mahogany writing and dove into the material. I was ready to become an artist. It didn't take long. I'm a scanner rather than a reader.

Rushing past cave paintings and medieval religious stuff, I discovered old masters and new masters that looked like old masters. I scanned dozen of books that didn't impress much. But then I came upon what I had been looking for, a book on Abstract Expressionism.

I paraphrase what I felt the book's first principle to be—feeling is the new thinking. It was something Berg or Hong or my mother might have said. According to the book's author, a professor from Yale who no doubt possessed unassailable historical grasp, the feeling-thinking "swap" began with a fellow named Mutt who hung a urinal at a show, insisting it was art. My kind of guy.

I had found my métier, and consulted more books, reading the who's, what's, why's, and where's concerning Abstract Expressionism. I shouldn't brag, but if you were to ask me about the differences between Arshille Gorky and Willem DeKooning, I could fill the better part of an hour with enough loose tidbits about these men to chase you from the room. I read somewhere that Abstract Expressionists used a technique known as "flinging paint" and instant art-combustions went off in my head. Flinging paint was something I knew I could do, and within a month I was expert.

Now, officially a suffering artist, I naturally spent a great deal of time in the bar next door.

The bar next door's name was Clodhoppers and we instantly fell in love.

. . . .

Berg's mastery at social intercourse was, like mine, given shine by his ability to make things up that sounded fresh and vaguely plausible. "Plausibility is sanity," I remember him once saying as an example of what he meant; that is, it meant nothing.

"Plausibility is mostly a matter of vocal insinuation and eyebrow manipulation. Always be reading your audience," he said. "Find out what they want to hear, then let them hear it. Let them be your enthusiasm."

Wisdom. Pure wisdom.

I practiced being plausible by being Berg-like when chatting with the fairer sex, mostly by quoting experts I'd invented on the spot.

"Karl Josef Kline-Weltenhausen is a mentor," I'd say to the Clodhopper chat-mate, generally a well-endowed Barbie doll. (Berg was a major dog when it came to the fairer sex, and I was no slouch in that category either, though a fledgling in comparison.) "I can't be alone in believing him to be the foremost post-Dada Executionist painting today."

"Wow," my chat-mate would say.

I'd then lay a hand on her arm and whisper, "It was Karl Josef who taught me the meaning of green."

Three classic subjects are available to painters: landscape, still life, and nudes. For reasons I shouldn't have to explain, I chose nudes. Landscapes require much discrete looking. Not only do you have to find just the right light, but you have to hike for miles to find it. Still life's are equally boring. Gee, wow, it's a pear next to another pear. No, it was nudes for me. If I couldn't paint one, I could at least enjoy their poses.

I discovered that nudes never fail to challenge the artist's eye. That's because a nude is constantly alive. She or he (in the spirit of full disclosure, while current fashion requires me to give male nude models equal billing, I have never employed one) is an extremely difficult object to paint, particularly when, like me, you tend to become entwined with them. I found entwinement helpful, you may not.

Unfortunately, my model would expect to see what I'd done. And they expected something that somewhat resembled her. Few models of the sort I chose were aficionados of the abstract. Most preferred pears next to other pears. My method included a lot of obliteration, slashing and scumbling. Told I was exciting to watch work—I referred to myself as an "athletic artist" even though I can't throw a ball—I would raise my hands into the air to indicate completion. Victory! It rarely took me more than ten minutes to do one. My subject, then draped in one of three Turkish terry cloth robes kept for such purposes, would snuggle up and ask, "Is that me? It looks like dog retch."

I'd comfort them by whispering, "It's your soul wearing a disguise." Or, if that didn't lure her to the Trampoline, I'd turn lecturer, one of Berg's favored techniques.

"Classical drawing has been long discredited, as Kline-Weltenhausen and the other Executionist's clearly proved." I'd stare into her eyes until just before it became uncomfortable, then say, "I think that still stands. What they did—and I am a follower of such procedures, as you can see by how I manage my markings—was to employ what Karly—Sorry, Karly is what Kline-Weltenhausen's friends call him—anyway, I follow what Karly first referred to in his famous article in Fine Arts Quarterly, as 'anti-line.'"

At this point, while measuring the vapidity of my muse, I'd ask, "You do understand, yes?" They invariably nodded yes, the naked beauties, their eyes wide with captivation.

Drawing things to a close, I'd say, "Painting things that look like actual things is ... well, you might as well be...a photographer!" I felt it important to sneer the word "photographer" in a slightly harsh, disapproving tone, like one might use when saying "pedophile".

Then I'd end with a flourish, leaning toward her: "Photographic drawing is like a woman (pause for effect) who cannot handle her man!"

. . . .

"Hi," Celine Pelligrano said when meeting me on the first floor landing of Old Admin's interior stairwell, an umbilical cord of concrete that joined the structure's lower organisms to me. It had been six months since I moved into Old Admin's penthouse. I knew few residents other than Celine. Thirty-ish, Celine was a sculptor perpetually covered in white dust. She was in front of her studio door as I passed her on the landing. She juggled a box of plaster while searching her pockets for her key.

Celine had me figured out. She looked at me with eyes that said, "Sure, I might flirt with you if weren't such a drunken, useless scumbag."

Did I frighten her? Perhaps. Did she frighten me? Absolutely.

Once, I mistakenly called her a sculptress and she corrected me, putting her hands on her hips and snarling, "That's sculptor." After that, I tended to avoid her. If you like being corrected after an honest attempt at being accurate, then good luck. Who can trust a women who does't appreciate the appellation of "ess?" The suffix is used by gentleman to celebrate of the differences between the sexes, not a rude slur. It's very off-putting being told your language is loose. It's like being told your zipper is down when it is merely broken.

"Plaster," I said courteously. "Cool."

Celine stood no more than 4' 10" and had orange-red hair that exploded from her head. Its spongy aura was roughly the same shape and width of her hips and together they made up sixty percent of her body mass. She must have terrorized children who came upon her suddenly in grocery store aisles.

Still, Celine wasn't bad looking after making allowances for her extreme elfishness and bouffant lunacy. And she was pleasant to watch as she walked away. Sadly, she was also immensely intelligent, meaning though she had the buttocks of a muse, she was strictly off limits for me.

"Are you going to show with us?" she shouted after me as I ascended the stairs leading to my lair. "I'm organizing it."

"If I can," I replied, having no intention of doing so. "I'll let you know." I carried a bag of pretzels and a twelve-pack of Bernie's beer and was anxious to tear into them.

I came to believe that Old Admin artists tended to be like dogs and children. That is, they had profound head-petting and coo-speak needs. For artists like Celine Pelligrano, being in a show—which they pronounce with a capital S—must satisfy some fetal need for succor and undivided attention. It's like your dog pooping on your Armenian rug, believing you'll love him for it.

A show is fundamentally about money, which no artist claims to be after. And yet money is all they talk about. Artists and gallerists never talk about how to make your wrist flick just so or why the color wheel never goes out of fashion. No, they talk about money. And the reason they talk about money is because money is art's only measure. The artist, the gallery operator and the collector, all ask the same question as does the art snob who just rolled in from the street. "How much?"

Money is the glue that keeps them all together. How else can they know if an artist is any good?

Should you still not agree, try this experiment. Settle onto your favorite barstool, making sure to sit next to someone you've never met before. Begin a pleasant exchange with them, then find a way to suggest to them that you are a painter. When your mark—forgive me, I fall easily into old habits—when your new bar mate says, "How interesting, do you show?" you'll instantly understand what I'm talking about. You can see it in their eyes. What they most wish to hear is that they are in the presence of a successful artist. And that success is endowed by money, as explained by the second most asked question in the art world, "How many have you sold?"

Most people are totally incapable of making any judgment about art unless they first know what others think. And the only way they can know how someone thinks about art is by knowing how much they paid for it.

For the standard artist, a show is not merely a show. It's an opportunity to put a price on their gigantic self-regard. Also, showing is what artists do instead of flashing strangers. "Hey, look at this."

Attending a show is like attending a grand ball, except that the show generally takes place in cramped hallway with bad lighting. You are forced to pass the artist's oeuvre on your way to the table where they've put the boxed wine. Nearby, the gallerist lurks wearing an oily smile and possibly a snazzy scarf. It is all about allure for them, as it is for most species of reptiles. Come hither, sweet meal.

Art shows, in fact, are so self-promoting that even art forgers are embarrassed to be associated with them. But they are an advertising executive's dream. "Nine out of ten dentists recommend this show." It is perhaps cruel to note this, but most people of the sort I am describing—at least most of those I met—cannot distinguish between being creative and being dull. They all marched to the same tarnished fife.

How well I understood this—was I not also this person? This faker? Humanity, for us deceivers, is about another's experience, not our own. Unable to recognize our shallowness, we adopt ad hoc rules such as Hong's Moral as guides. Thereafter, we pretend to possess depth, uttering all sorts of meaningless nonsense about the imagination and the creative life.

Human beings are such frauds. No wonder I love us.

. . . .

Old Admin's artists were comprised primarily of two sorts: men who did not bathe and women who did not bathe. What kinds of art they produced held zero interest for me—as long as they stayed in their sties. Nevertheless, there was one artist I did find interesting. I seldom saw him, but noticed he carried himself with an affected sense of superiority. This is generally the mark of a charismatic failure and I liked him immediately.

Once, while in the alley tossing some paintings into the dumpster, I saw Celine talking with him. They were next to the building. Her head bobbed like a mad radish. Seeing me, she waved me to come over. I eagerly did and she introduced us.

His name was Selden. Selden's studio was on the first floor on the alley side of the building. Like me, he was of average height and weight. The average man, having no natural advantages, is forced to evolve. My evolutionary trait was being full of it. Selden's were wearing a black Kangol cap, white coveralls, and stinking of pot.

One day—it was raining and I was tending a screeching hangover due to winning a bet at Clodhoppers regarding Jameson consumption—I heard a rap against my studio's oak door. I would have ignored it, as I usually did, but the knock was especially firm and unyielding. I dragged myself from the Trampoline and trudged to the door. I unbolted and opened it—and lo and behold—it was Selden.

"May an artist ask a favor of another?" he said.

His elocution was pronounced, exact, making me suspect that Selden belonged to the same club of pretenders I did. But as we had only recently been introduced, I was guarded. Nodding acquaintance does not an immediate friendship make, particularly between artists whose egos hide true intentions.

"If I can," I said, quoting Berg. Berg said it a lot, adding "Wary promises are more comfortable on the soul."

"I'm about to have a painting session with my co-creator, Curley," Selden said. "And I've just realized that I've run out of white paint. You wouldn't happen to have some spare white lying around I could borrow, would you?"

Broadly speaking, borrowing is not something I approve. I prefer to give outright rather than lend. It is an ethical position I shared with Berg. Giving has finality. It is clean, over and done with. Lending, on the other hand, means you'll probably have to endure more time with the borrower than you may wish. It's a crap shoot. It's like I imagine collecting rents must be, forced to say, "Sorry, Grandma, if I don't get it by the end of the month, I'll call the Sheriff." And it gets worse. The idiot sub-sheriff will take the opportunity of Grandma's broken hearing aid to claim she didn't follow orders, which is why they had to taser her. That leads to court cases and being punished for lying under oath. Who needs that? Thank God that was Dimple's problem, not mine.

"Sure, but please consider it a gift," I said to Selden, affecting magnanimity. "How about a tube of Titanium? Or flake white?"

"Actually, I was hoping you might have a bucket of white house paint. Exterior oil based, if you have it."

I was startled. How did Selden know I used oil based white house paint to cover over my nude paintings after waking and realizing they sucked? Oil based exterior house white was my preferred obliteration material. Had he rummaged my paintings in the dumpster? Did Celine tell him? (Of all the Old Admin's tenants only Celine had actually been into my studio, a judgmental lapse I never allowed to be repeated. The lingering spiritual effects on rooms recently visited by overly intelligent girls makes my head swirl in eddies of self-doubt; I believe it's an allergy.)

"In fact I do have some oil based white exterior," I said.

We stood, momentarily unmoving, two men assessing each other. Did I like Selden? Did he like me? Did either of us care? We were both painters after all, I reasoned, and I like to be host-like to fellow artists in need. That is unless they are swarthy pigs or sows that avoid bathing.

"I've quite a bit, in fact. You're welcome to as much as you'd like." I invited Selden to enter my sanctum sanctorum.

"Whoa," Selden said, looking around. "I heard you had great digs, but this..."

I went to the storage locker behind the Japanese crane mural and retrieved a gallon of exterior house white and, bringing it to set on the floor beside him, saying graciously, "How's this?"

"Thank you, kind sir," Selden said, picking up the can of paint. I stepped towards my door, grasping the doorknob, then turning to him, intending to express my appreciation for his dropping by. But Selden didn't move. I gave him an "is there something else?" look with raised left eyebrow (I raise a left eyebrow to men, right for the ladies).

He seemed almost shy, as if his mind were stammering, and it took a moment for him to speak. "You know Celine, right?"

"Not really. We chat sometimes."

"You know she's having a show next month? Actually, it's for everyone."

"Right." Was Selden her spy?

"Just wondering, then ... are you going to show? I am." Selden jutted his jaw out, proudly and defiant, like Mussolini before he was hung.

"No. I do not show," I said, responding with an arrogant chin jut of my own. "I paint."

Was this rude? I can be rude, I know. I inherited that trait from my mother. But it is not a particularly big worry, as, like my mother, I care little about what others think of me. Beside that, as Berg would say, "When you have money to throw around, a lack of manners is just a careless oversight, not a venial sin."

If Selden felt I had attempted to one-up him, he showed no outward recognition of it.

"Understandable," he said with an unaffected tone of goodwill. His manner was generous, even warm. "I don't normally show either. I'm just doing it because Celine asked me to."

He stood, perhaps waiting for me to speak. I didn't. Something was on his mind and I waited for it to find itself. It was, as the gamesmen say, his play. After a brief moment of eye jousting, he said, "The thing is, she'd appreciate all of us showing. You know? Artists supporting artists. Supporting each other."

"Ah," I said, nodding my understanding. Selden clearly had the hots for Celine. She was his Venus flytrap, he her naive fly. I wanted to say, "Yes, you are attracted to her because that's how God tricks us. Trust me, I would know. I too had a girlfriend once whose name began with a C. But if you desire a tiny russet puffball with a perky bottom who likes to show all the time, who am I to object?"

But of course I didn't say this. Why? Because I liked the manly thrust of Selden's jaw. Also, I'd seen empty cases of beer by his door, so knew he was a man of principle.

In England when you call someone mate, he could be a guy whose foot you just stepped while waiting for a bus. In New Rotterdam, if you called someone your mate, divorce lawyers would be circling the waters waiting for you to hit bottom. But with Selden, I didn't feel mate-ness happening, rather a chummy partnership. Like me, Selden was a butt man, which triggered feelings of bonhomie. So, if gazing at Celine's tiny bottom sent the nerve-endings of Selden's balls aflutter, I could only respect that. Some silent, male code requires such.

I stuck out my hand. He took it. His palm was warm and his fingers long. We looked each other in the eye, neither of us flinching until satisfied the electricity we shared was not homoerotic.

"I will certainly think about showing," I said, making my equivocation appear to be an agreement. Berg called this "saying no with a yes."

"Thanks," he said. "I told Celine you'd probably do it. She and Curley didn't think you would, but I told them you had the look of a man who understands what painting is all about." Was he man-charming me? I didn't know and didn't care. It was simply nice to hear someone say something nice about me. Nice is frequently nice, no two ways about it.

He approached the door I held open for him, but stopped before going through it. "Say, I have an idea."

"What's that, Selden?"

"You should come watch us Oreo."

"I'm not really into cookies, old man. Baked goods give me gas."

"No, no, not cookies."

Was Selden talking about a three-way with two black chicks? Had I misread him? Was this Curley person his photographer?

Selden, seeing my confusion, said, "It's just a painting thing we do. I invented it."

My left eyebrow rose.

"Hey, you know how it is. I'm an Abstract painter. Invention is what we do."

"Flinging paint?" I asked.

"Exactamundo. Flinging paint," Selden said, his head tossing back with a laugh that reminded me somewhat of Berg's. It was natural and unforced, like a regal bird of prey might appear to a gauzy-eyed environmentalist before it ate a fledgling's head.

Honor is a difficult word, I use it with reservation, for there is little remotely honorable about me. But in that moment—that finding-a-new-friend moment—I felt Selden's invitation to be honorably given. And I realized that while I had plenty of drinking pals, none of them were painting pals. I stared at Selden for a moment, collecting my composure.

I said with surprising sincerity. "I accept."

Something near my heart fluttered. Was this to be the first page of a new chapter in my life as a painter? And though I was excited, I also was becalmed, for I knew Selden to be a drinking man. As Berg said many times, "Empty Bernie's never lie."

"What time?" I asked.

"Now is as good a time as any," Selden said. "Curley's almost here." His lips formed an affable grin, and I took it to be a sign of hedonism.

"Evoe," I shouted, instinctively. Selden's eyes broadened with glad surprise.

"Evoe" he shouted back, his voice box vibrant, tenor toned. What ho, we were fellow Bacchanalians. Selden put a hand on my shoulder like we were fraternity brothers.

"Wait a second," I said, stopping at the door and reaching behind it to retrieve what I then held up for Selden's inspection. He smiled, nodding silent affirmation. I had been so excited by Selden's invitation to watch he and Curley and the Oreo that I almost forgot the quart of Jameson Select Reserve Black Barrel I had been saving for a special occasion.

When you are about to meet someone named Curley performing something called an Oreo, it qualifies as a special occasion.

. . . .

The size of Selden's live-work studio was shockingly small. Apparently, there were seven such studios. You'd think a manager would know this, but that was Dimple's territory, not mine. My job was merely to be Ambrose Berg's spendthrift.

The studio was fifteen feet deep and eighteen feet wide, with an eight foot ceiling. Selden had nailed a two-by-four against the far wall, upon which a sheet of plywood sat. Eye-balling it, I estimated the plywood to be about four feet on each side.

Selden noticed my interest, "Do you think management would mind?" He said it with boyish charm like he'd just been caught reading Playboy.

I smiled and said, "I'm sure the management appreciates tenants with imagination." We laughed. Just then a very short and chubby, prematurely bald man walked into the studio. It was Selden's co-creator, Curley. Selden introduced us and Curley went over to sit on Selden's folding futon mattress that did double duty as a chair.

The rest of the studio was filled with loose art supplies and cardboard boxes. I saw a hot plate with a sauce pan sitting on it caked with dried paint, mostly red. Dozens of wadded bags with McDonald and Subway logos on them overflowed a plastic trash can. In one corner of the room were a pile spent paint tubes. I did not see a fire extinguisher.

I found a sturdy box, moved it closer to the door and sat on it. "Now tell me about this Oreo thing."

Curley spoke. "It's the best, man. Powerful." I thought I detected an Australian accent.

"Where are you from, Curley?" I asked.

"Here. Devilbridge at first, but I live in town now."

"Uptown," Selden said, ribbing him.

"Well, if you call an apartment even shittier than this one uptown, I guess I'm uptown."

Selden informed Curley that I was the owner of Old Admin and Curley eyed me suspiciously.

"Actually, I only represent the owner," I corrected. "But he's a good guy, so no worries."

"Cool," Curley said, reaching into his coat pocket and withdrew from it a joint. He lit it and inhaled. As he exhaled he whispered "Oreo" without breathing.

Selden stood. "In this corner," he said as if announcing a boxing match, "is Curley the Surly, super middle-weight champion from Devilbridge." He pointed at Curley who raised his hands high like Ali. I love false bravado and so clapped wildly. Curley nodded appreciatively.

"And in the other corner," Selden said, "Drum roll, please." I dutifully bongoed the edge of my box. "Selden the Magnificent."

I applauded. Curley booed.

Selden and Curley each set a gallon can of exterior oil paint at their side. White for Selden, black for Curley. Selden reached into a cardboard box and pulled out two five-inch paint brushes. In the meantime, Curley found a roll of duct tape. They duct taped the brushes to each others hands, so that each hand appeared to have sprouted a beard. Curley's looked Amish.

When I mentioned my impression to Curley, he said, "ZZ Top, eat your heart out."

Selden turned to me again, saying, "You have the inebriation material ready, sir?"

"I do," I said, cracking open the Jamison Select Reserve Black Barrel and placing it on top of a piece of ratty luggage that appeared to serve as a coffee table. A sleeve of red plastic cups was laying on its side near my chair. I pulled three from the sleeve and placed them next to the Jameson bottle. I poured a couple of fingers of the magic elixir into each.

Selden said, "The rules of an Oreo are simple. Each painter is allowed one stroke of the brush, after which we take a swig. The Oreo is over when either one of us passes out...

Curley interjected, "Selden never passes out."

"...or agree the Oreo is completed."

Curley said, "Selden never agrees."

Selden said, "We usually just run out of paint." Curley shrugged compliance.

Several previous Oreos were stacked against the wall. "Why plywood?" I asked.

"They don't degrade," said Curley. "Conservationists love that."

I raised my plastic red cup. "To the Conservationists," They raised their cups and we toasted.

"To the Conservationists," we sang as one.

Selden turned toward Curley and said, "Age before beauty," Curley dipped his brush hand into his gallon of black paint, withdrawing it, then made a wide horizontal brush stroke across the top third of the plywood. He took a swig of Jameson.

Selden's subsequent white diagonal brushstroke partially covered Curley's move as he let his arm roam free over the surface of the plywood. I considered myself an athletic painter, but Selden was the real thing. He seemed to be dancing at the easel.

They went at it like this, turn by turn, black and white rejecting or merging, covering the other's marks, taking swigs, creating something new. Once Curley performed a black slash worthy of Tree Drunk Soldier Hand but Selden deftly turned it into a portrait of a haughty amoeba with long gray sideburns.

And so it went for roughly two hours until most of the Jamison's and several beers were gone. At that point, Selden threw up his hands, signaling victory. "Selden the Magnificent wins again," he proclaimed. Curley did not disagree and grabbed the last Bernie's.

Selden implored me to give the work a name.

"Delighted," I said, rising from my box to examine the work briefly before turning to face them.

"Hong's Moral," I said.

"Evoe," shouted Selden. "Hong's Moral it is."

Curley grinned, downed his Bernie's in one gulp, and lit up a joint.

. . . .

Celine's flier advertised "an art gala, an evening of remarkable creations displayed by remarkable artists." Alas, two remarkable's don't make a gala. Of the dozen or so Old Admin artists who availed themselves of the opportunity to show, only Celine's art work was impressive enough for me to actually ponder it. I didn't understand her work one bit, but could tell it was expertly done, featuring lots of intersecting circles and squares with rounded curves. I picked up one of her handouts, but immediately put it back after seeing the word "feminist" in the first sentence. Irrespective of her gender focus, she was clearly the most talented of Old Admin's artists.

The least impressive work was by an incompetent woman named Clough. She claimed to be "Neo-Calderian," and I doubted Calder would feel honored. Clough's art was to turn paperclips into the shape of circus animals, most of which looked like otters. She hung them from brackets attached to the wall. I spent about five seconds looking at them from every angle, until deciding they were not circus animals at all, not even otters. They were paperclips with spinal disorders. All were curled into uncomfortable-looking fetal positions. Clough had no written instruction regarding what her art meant, my guess was inner pain.

Next to Clough was Abe Skloon. Skloon's talent didn't "combine science and art" as his promotional information claimed. Below his bio, in which he thanked his four grandparents by name, including their middle initials, Skloon wrote, "Skloon engages interior dialogues with the outer world" and that "he seeks art that enfolds time." Yeah, right. Skloon welded plastic junk together with a glue gun. Skloon reminded me of an old adage my mother often used: "Are you out of your fucking mind?"

Art can be a wonderfully fraudulent exercise, one of the chief reasons I felt born to it. Of course, there is good fraudulence and bad fraudulence. Skloot represented the latter. One piece, entitled "Beachcomber" was random blue plastic pieces glued together and sprayed with polyethylene infused with sand. Skloot, as his handout further explained, was a proud graduate of the New Rotterdam School District's "Children's Response to Art Program."

Another artist named Christian had as his subject matter ferns. His technique was to pick ferns and coat them in a "proprietary" solution he had invented. He'd press the ferns between sheets of newspaper until the fern's image was artistically transferred to the front page news. Christian called his work "Ferncals." I actually rather enjoyed the Ferncals. They possessed an admirable ambiance of falsity. Unfortunately, I never had a chance to meet Christian as he rarely came out of his studio unless it was to collect ferns. Where he got them, no one knew, though the scuttlebutt was that he cultivated them near the New Rotterdam dump.

Berg considered false modesty "an attempt to bullshit God. As if they think the mystery of life could learn a thing or two." I was reminded of this when introduced to Xavier, my choice to win Old Admin's biggest ego award. His reputation as being impressive preceded him, though the estimation quickly eroded in his presence.

When you're not very good at something, you develop compensatory skills. For instance, if the truth confuses you, you learn to lie. If you're bad at carrying on intelligent conversations, you develop the ability to stare into space with the gauzy look of a Pre-Raphaelite. Likewise, if you are a lousy artist, as Xavier was, you talk about yourself endlessly and eat Brie from other people's plates.

Xavier had no last name. Like Elvis and Cher, he didn't need more names trailing in his wake of wonderfulness. When I met him, it was brief. Selden introduced us.

Selden: "Hey, Xavier. How's it hangin.'"

Xavier: "You know me, Selden. I'm cool."

Selden: "By the way, I'd like you to meet a friend. He owns this place."

Xavier (to me): "You own Old Admin?"

Me: "Well, not personally. I'm just the owner's representative."

Xavier: "So you only own it impersonally?"

Me: "That's funny. You should do comedy."

Xavier: "Wait a minute, you represent Berg? The Berg who started the New Rotterdam University Art Museum?"

Me: "He asked me not to discuss that." It was the first I'd heard of the New Rotterdam University Art Museum, but didn't let on that it was news to me.

Xavier: "Why not, it's cool."

Me: "I know, but he'd rather be known for art than wealth."

Xavier seemed flummoxed by my answer, his face turning a weird shade of pink. The green sweater he was wearing made the pink pinker. I knew that from reading about color theory in Wikipedia. I turned and left. Xavier might have been wittier than me and I didn't want to find out.

Later, Selden told me that Xavier used to be an art teacher in Kansas, but came to New Rotterdam after he had a dream that he was leading people to the Promised Land.

"He said that?"

"He wrote it. It's on the wall in the 2nd floor uni-sex bathroom."

"There's a uni-sex bathroom here? Why didn't I know this?"

. . . .

Selden and Curley's "Hong's Moral" was positioned next to Celine's work. I was biased, of course, but it was truly magnificent, no doubt the hit of the show as people were milling around it constantly. It didn't hurt that it was next to the table with the wine on it.

"It looks like Franz Kline married Phyllis Diller," said one inebriant.

"Nah," slurred her friend, "its from the Exorcist."

I thought "Hong's Moral" beautiful, though it had one significant change. It wasn't signed by Selden or Curley. It was signed by Ambrose Berg (by Selden's hand).

Ambrose wanted to be an artist, and now he was.

Impressed by Selden's and Curley's artistic methodology, I had offered them jobs in the same manner as Ambrose Berg had offered me a job. Selden and Curley were instantly employees of Ambrose Berg Enterprises, LLC as "art consultants." It was a maneuver I knew Berg would appreciate. "Mimicking good works is a good work in itself," he once said.

Later, when telling Dimple of my new hires, I handed him a photographic print of "Hong's Moral." Dimple said he'd forward the information to Berg.

For the next month, I continued my Bergian pursuit of the artistic life by avoiding Old Admin in favor of Clodhoppers. Most art making is mental, I reasoned, and there is nothing better for one's mental life than a shot of Jameson.

Then, one day, Dimple was at my door.

I invited him in, which he accepted warily. Once inside, he looked around and shook his head in dismay. Then he handed me a small box. It was wrapped in white silk, with white silk ribbons and a large white silk bow. Inside the box were business cards indicating my new title was "Senior Executive Special Assistant."

"And this," said Dimple, handing me a linen envelope. It was a handwritten note from Berg. "We did it!" he wrote. "Finally, I'm an artist." It warmed my heart to see some influences of Tree Drunk Soldier Hand in his script.

"And this," Dimple said again. He gave me a folded piece of paper, then stood with slouched attention like a manservant. It was a check made out to me in the amount of $100,000.

"Wow," I said. "I should do this more often."

"Indeed," said Dimple, his voice wavering between admiration and derision. "I think Ambrose has found his man."

. . . .

Several weeks later, I opened my door following a knock. It was Dimple with an ashen look on his face.

"I have some very troubling news," he said.

I suspected the worst. "Don't tell me Berg is dead?"

"No, not quite."

"Injured?"

"Not specifically."

"What then?" I implored. Dimple was not one to get to the point. He was a born stammerer who had developed into a ditherer.

"There is a legal matter," Dimple said.

"I'm being tossed out? Are the cops on their way?"

"No, you're safe," Dimple said.

My mood lightened as the cloud of unknowing lifted. If I wasn't losing my position, what did troubling news have to do with me? "Then what's the problem?" I asked.

"I'm afraid Ambrose has gotten himself into a bit of a legal fix," Dimple said, brushing past me and sitting on one of two Parda swivel chairs I had recently purchased.

I sat in the other Parda. Leaning forward, I said, "Give it to me straight, Dimple. What's up?"

"This is a really nice chair," Dimple said.

"Yes it is. What's going on, Dimple?"

Dimple sank into the chair. It seemed to swallow him whole. "As you may know," he said, "Ambrose has many unusual friends." He gave me an arch look.

"Yes," I said. "He told me once the unusual was usual for him."

"Indeed," Dimple said, shaking his head while looking into his lap. "But this one takes the cake."

I didn't feel like prodding Dimple anymore, so sat quietly, waiting for his denouement.

"One of Ambrose's friends got him tied up in a smuggling operation."

"Drugs," I said. "I knew it."

"No, no, not drugs, "Dimple said, adding hemming and hawing to his stammer and dither. He fidgeted in the Parda.

"Then what? What is it?"

Dimple straightened his spine and looked directly in my eye. "Bonobo semen," he said.

"Bonobo semen? What's that?"

"The semen of apes. It is apparently the basis of an aphrodisiac. I believe Swedes use it. Or Norwegians, perhaps."

"Wow," I said. "Does it work?"

Dimple did not answer but rose and walked over to my desk. On it he placed a folder, and from it withdrew several papers. He carefully laid them next to each other. All were flecked with yellow post-it notes.

"Here," Dimple said. "Sign where indicated and initial where indicated."

"Why? What's going on?"

"We are transferring ownership of Old Admin to you."

"Really? I'm going to own this place?"

Dimple's personality dithered with itself for several long seconds until he said, "We need to unemcumber Ambrose. Free him up a bit."

"I'm all for freedom," I said.

I signed and initialed the papers and Dimple left. I was now the owner of Old Admin. The first thing I did was ask myself what would Berg do? What would he want me to do? For the next month I sought Selden and Curley's advice with multiple Bernies. Finally, I had a plan.

I sold Old Admin to a cabal of lawyers and moved to San Miguel de Allende, Mexico, taking Selden and Curley with me.

Artists, you can't stop them, you can only join them in pretending to know what they are doing.

The Magical Smelt

"Dammit," Florabunda said with a sigh of acceptance. She looked to the heavens and tossed back her regal red hair. It was dark purple, a mix of heirloom tomato and sloe. "The gambler's fate," she said, holding up the losing Lotto ticket to show her husband, Grampie. They sat facing each other at the kitchen table. "You'd think a good woman like me could catch a break." She stared at the ticket, made a face of mock disappointment, ripped it in half, and smiled.

"A waste of money," Grampie said. Balding, big and stout, with gnarled knuckles and a loving grin, he had the TV remote in one hand while petting their cat, Sluggo, with the other.

Grampie and Florabunda Flatt, Jr., had lived in the Del Vista Del Apartments for their entire married life, thirty four years. The Del Vista Del was three interlocked stucco buildings that resembled cardboard boxes in New Rotterdam's North Slope neighborhood. Florabunda often said they were "near Lancaster," because Lancaster, the tonier neighborhood, was just four blocks up the street. Four blocks the other way was Smelt Field, home of New Rotterdam's professional baseball team, the Smelt. Grampie managed the Smelt, as had his father, Grampie Flatt, Sr.

"I think it's wonderful you followed in your dad's footsteps," Florabunda once told Grampie while they watched the Mariners play the As. "You get to have his history running through your blood all the time. That's fantastic." She finished the last of her hotdog and said, "Wow. I love thinking like that."

They met at a Smelt game. It was during New Rotterdam's annual Begonia Festival. Florabunda was a Begonia Princess, and Grampie, then an assistant clubhouse manager had escorted her to her seat in the front row behind the home team dugout. Grampie, twenty-two, said to sixteen year-old Princess Florabunda, "I like your hair. It's like soft fire." They were married three years later and honeymooned in Boise.

Florabunda began working at New Rotterdam Electric & Gas soon after their marriage. Beginning as an office assistant in the utility company's Customer Service Department, Florabunda was now the department manager. A month after her promotion, Grampie earned his own promotion after Smelt manager, Grampie

Sr., dropped dead of a heart attack during a losing argument with an umpire.

Grampie and Florabunda ordered steaks and martinis that night at Clodhoppers. They toasted Grampie's dad, and Florabunda noted, "You can't bring the dead back, you can only go forward with life." Florabunda was a natural philosopher, a trait Grampie deeply admired. No wonder they promoted her, he thought.

They clicked glasses and toasted themselves, "Here's to being in charge."

When Grampie's mother died of natural causes several years later, Grampie and Florabunda reprised their steak and martini dinner. Grampie raised his martini and said, "Both gone now. I think they went the way they wanted."

"Yeah," said Florabunda, "One with his boots on, and one who hung on til she couldn't nag no more."

. . . .

Everyone loved Florabunda. Men ogled her constantly. Most lost focus once she entered their full periphery. A born beauty, she was curvy and full bosomed from the moment she entered puberty. By the time she became a Begonia Princess, her posture was elegant, with exquisite, proportioned legs. Her nose was said to be perfect. Yet, for all her physical charms, it was Florabunda's style that captured people's attention.

A member of Nordstrom's Nordy Club, Florabunda adorned herself in current upscale fashion. Her trademark was her vibrant use of color, especially with her hair. She let it express itself by being always freshly dyed, always with a classy hue. Mahogany or pink tangerine one month, burgundy with a hint of burnt orange the next. "It has a mind of its own," she said. "I don't argue with it."

Florabunda Flatt was New Rotterdam Electric & Gas Customer Service Department's most chic manager in history. Grampie knew he was a lucky man when it came to his wife. He told her all the time that she was "a million times better than baseball." That meant a lot to Florabunda, given baseball was all Grampie thought about. She felt equally lucky to be with him. She once had a dream of them lashed together on the mast of a ship, back to back, holding hands.

During one election season, a girlfriend, the wife of an armchair philosopher with a bad attitude, made a disparaging remark about Grampie, calling him "Mr. Grumpy." Florabunda said, "Well, at least he votes his good conscience, not his bile like some men I know." Then she struck a pose like a movie star on the front of a Hollywood magazine.

As a child, Florabunda had watched old cowboy movies with her grandpa, who said all the good movies were made in Utah. Her grandpa owned a travel trailer and said Utah was the most beautiful state in the Union. He regaled little Florabunda with stories of travel-trailing through Utah, bouncing her on his knee, saying, "Here comes a road bump. Better be ready."

Ever since, it was Florabunda's fondest dream to get an RV and head for Utah.

Her hands fluttered above her dark sloe tress, shaping it with air. "We should go to Utah for sure when we retire. We really should. You'd love it, sweetheart. I know you would."

Grampie wasn't good at math, but he could do basic addition and subtraction. And that was easy because only two numbers mattered. The first number was that saving money was not in Florabunda's DNA, and the other number was the fact the Smelt not only played like crap, they paid like it too. Old baseball managers don't get pensions, they get forgotten. An RV heading for Utah? It was

Florabunda's pipe dream, though he'd never tell her that. Grampie didn't like pipe dreams, they made him think about the future.

Managing the Smelt was his dream as a youngster, but now it was reality. How long could he manage the Smelt? He often felt younger than he was, but the calendar quickly reminded him he was already fifty-four. His father died at sixty-four.

Grampie figured the Grimaldis, who owned the Smelt, wouldn't fire him. Who else would take the job? There aren't many baseball vagabonds whose dream it is to manage the worst team in baseball. In a world that prizes certainty, the only certainty about the Smelt was that they would lose again.

Florabunda had a nice pension and a small IRA, enough to ensure they wouldn't starve in old age. But Grampie knew Florabunda would never quit the Nordy Club without a gun battle. And her Lotto habit sure wasn't going to stop. Florabunda bought Lotto tickets daily, ritually from the grocery on Washcon and Draper. It's her money, Grampie reasoned. She can do what the hell she wants with it. All he could do was grumble? "Makes no sense. It's like an intentional walk with the bases loaded."

"You can make fun of me all you want, honey. But I'm telling you," Florabunda said. "One of these days, I'm going to hit the big one."

Grampie said, "Yeah, that's what Bang Bang always says."

Bang Bang was the veteran Smelt center fielder known for his ability to strike out with flair.

. . . .

In 1927, the New Rotterdam city dump had reached capacity. Roaring Twenties junk overflowed its bounds and the air around it turned foul. Children pinched their noses at the dinner table and told each other, "Phew, you stink." Native plants in the area began to die. People started coming down with vertigo. New filth evolved from existing filth.

A new dumpsite was the solution. A suitable location found on the out-skirts of Piccolo, the village fifteen miles east of New Rotterdam. "Perfect," New Rotterdam's mayor enthused. "Piccolo's downwind most of the year."

But what to do with the old dump site? It wouldn't just molder away, not just disappear with the wave of a wand. An answer arrived in the person of a snooty fellow who said his grandfather had made a fortune selling Alaskans shovels. The man had been educated in England and wouldn't stop talking about it. He announced that he intended to turn the old dump into a cricket field. He purchased the dump from the city, covered it with dirt and had grass seed strewn over it. He advertised for "manly, health-given sportsmen" to join The Royal New Rotterdam Cricket Club, "The Most Premier Cricket Club West of the Mississippi."

It did not go well. New Rotterdam's manly, health-given sportsmen were not, alas, cricket people. Most had never even heard of cricket. They thought a Cricket Club was a bunch of guys raising grasshoppers. Rather, like the rest of America, New Rotterdammers were baseball people. Besides that, the cricket promoter was a fraudster, which didn't help matters. His checks bounced and the sheriff was called to escort him out of town. Within weeks, the proposed cricket field reverted to city ownership and its grass died. Once a dump, always a dump.

A month later, the mayor's daughter, while playing near the old dump, found a boot with a human toe in it. Before long, a modest bond measure to clean up the former dump site was passed. The mayor made it a major issue in his reelection campaign. When pressed on his plans for the property, the mayor, utilizing publicity to his best advantage, had said, "I don't care what it becomes, just so long as it doesn't include toes." By the following summer the old cricket dump had been transformed into a flat, grassy field without hidden body parts. People began referring to it as The Pasture and it was the exact right size for baseball games.

Ad hoc games require ad hoc rules. For teams playing on The Pasture, a ball ending up in the gorse in left field was an automatic homer, and a ball stuck in the mud bank bordering center and right field was a triple. And so for several seasons the boys of summer played ball on The Pasture, enjoying baseball, immune to unsightly body parts.

The mayor, as it happened, was a tight-fisted bastard. It took many years before New Rotterdam was able to be rid of him. Regarding The Pasture, he refused to pay for its upkeep, saying the city had done its job by removing the stink and toes, the rest was up to citizens. "If they want to play ball on that field, they can damn well take care of it," he said, endearing himself to those New Rotterdam voters most likely to shout, "Get off my lawn."

It was the New Rotterdam High School baseball team who took on the challenge. Several of them were also 4-H men, so they had access to a small hay sickle you could tow behind a truck. They'd play for a couple of weeks, mow, then play again. Mow, play, mow, play. Then one summer a Boy Scout troop cleaned up the scrub bushes and erected a fence from scrap plywood. The following year another troop filled in the mud bank because one of their fathers owned New Rotterdam Sand and Gravel.

Slowly, season by season, game by game, The Pasture became New Rotterdam's primary baseball field of pipe dreams.

....

In 1934, The Western Baseball Association was looking to expand its league from five to six. As it happened, willing movers-and-shakers in New Rotterdam showed interest. That interest became an offer to build a road past a parcel of land the mayor owned in exchange for The Pasture. No one objected because no one knew, and a backroom deal was struck. Professional baseball had arrived in New Rotterdam.

A baseball stadium had to be build. Of course, as always, financing was an issue, and New Rotterdam baseball investors were as skinflint-y as the mayor. A committee was authorized to look into the matter and, after three days of consultation at the Rosebud Tavern they recommended hiring an architect. The only architect of note in New Rotterdam was Augustus Rochambeau. Rochambeau, then in his 70s, had earned his architectural stripes by designing elaborate outhouses for New Rotterdam's nouveau rich during the 1890s. As indoor plumbing increasingly became fashionable, Rochambeau transformed himself into a commercial building architect, a ubiquitous presence in the New Rotterdam building scene. His largest and most famous project was the Washcon Bridge, a bridge the Tribune boasted, "might look like a hedgehog, but it has more steel in its spine than any New Rotterdam building has a right to."

The job of building the baseball stadium was Rochambeau's for the taking, and he took it. Putting foot to spade at the ribbon cutting ceremony, Rochambeau read from the script he was given, "It'll be just as good as the House that Ruth Built." New Rotterdam baseball fans went delirious, celebrating long into the night until a volunteer fireman set a shed on fire.

A lottery was conducted to name the new team. School children were given tiny pieces of paper resembling the type found inside fortune cookies and asked to pencil in their suggestions. 513 suggestions found their way to baseball officials. The suggestions were then put into a burlap bag and a Begonia Princess was asked to reach into the bag and pick one suggestion out.

"Smelt," the Princess yelled.

"What the hell is a Smelt?" shouted someone.

No one thought to answer that question and the name Smelt prevailed. A commercial artist, at first befuddled when attempting to draw a mascot representing blast furnace detritus, finally drew a fish wearing a baseball hat with a mitt on its right fin. It was called Fishhook.

In the months surrounding construction, baseball was all New Rotterdammers talked about. Posters of famous baseball players were featured in every storefront and in the hallways of every public school. It became the fad to name boy children, Babe, and the girls, Ruth.

Architect Rochambeau was feted by the city with a parade down Washcon Avenue. As he sat atop the back seat of a new Ford Roadster during the parade, Rochambeau waved grandly to the crowd. He wore a camel topcoat and a wide brimmed hat. Streamers flew around his head and he caught one of them. He shook it at the adoring fans who lined the street. As they cheered, Rochambeau turned to the mayor who was riding with him and asked, "Is baseball the one you bounce or kick?"

Smelt Field, once completed, did not look like the House that Ruth Built. Rather, it looked like the Washcon Bridge had lost its bolts and collapsed in on itself. Decades later, before he was fired for cause by New Rotterdam University, Archtecture and Justice Professor H. I. Talewonkus claimed Frank Gehry was inspired by Smelt Field.

As an adornment, four large black steel wires wove along Smelt Field's facade. They loomed above the main gate. Many arguments ensued over whether or not the ropes were for architectural or aesthetic purposes. To kids they looked like licorice laces, to adults like they were strangling themselves. The truth was that Rochambeau, as was the case with Washcon Bridge, received kickbacks from New Rotterdam Iron and Steel. As a result, he had lots of extra steel lying around. He had to get rid of it somehow. When asked about it by a Tribune reporter, Rochambeau said the black wires represented the intersection of sky and water; then, while suffering a coughing fit, he changed the subject.

·······

The New Rotterdam Smelt struggled from their very first pitch. Perennial losers throughout their history, the team, along with the stadium, was bought and sold by a succession of enthusiastic, rich hobbyists with more money than good sense. The owner of Ford Brother's Chevrolet bought the team only to sell it three months later, a victim of spousal support. A hardware store magnate bought it twice, after having sold it once to his useless nephew.

In late 1970, the New Rotterdam Smelt and Smelt Field were purchased by the Garibaldis. While the Garibaldis weren't baseball people, they were concessions people. Specifically, they owned Garibaldi's Clam Shacks, a dozen of which served Greater New Rotterdam.

"It's a growth opportunity," argued Ricardo Garibaldi, the eldest son who had a skill set appropriate for the Smelt: no hits, no runs, lots of errors. Ricardo later opened Clam Shacks near each baseball stadium in the Western Baseball Association. "Who doesn't like clams?" he said, "It's a no brainer." But of course, it was a brainer. Las Vegas Showstopper fans want slot machines, not clams. And Tempe Gila Monster fans don't eat clams, they eat rattlesnakes and lizards.

Midway in their tenure as owners of the Smelt, the Garibaldis installed a large neon sign over the front gate. When it worked, it spelled "CLAM BUCKETS GALORE," the same phrase blazoned across each Clam Shack bucket. In the annual "What's Worst About New Rotterdam" survey of New Rotterdam University students, the Garibaldi's sign was always in the top three, winning outright four years running.

"No one comes to the ballpark to watch the Smelt," claimed Gabriella Garibaldi, managing partner. "They come for clams and Bernie's beer. What's better than another Bernie's to wash down your clams? Nothing, that's what. And, of course, nine innings of clams and beer naturally leads to a Smelt Cone."

Alas, the Garibaldi clam empire was distressed. Twice in a dozen years, the local shellfish industry was decimated by a clam disease caused by a bacteria associated with algae. Kingfish Beach, where the Garibaldis harvested their clams, was the epicenter of the algae bloom. The Clam Shack franchise was barely staying afloat. And this meant the Smelt were yet again up for sale. Fortunately for the Garibaldis, they were early investors in Apple, so stupid decisions didn't faze them.

....

The Western Baseball Association had existed in various forms and combinations since 1924. In addition to the Smelt were the Eureka Bandits, the Arizona Gila Monsters, the Baker City Lodestars, the Daily City Tender Loins, and the Las Vegas Showstoppers.

Harvey Klunk, his massive head turned piebald by eczema, owned the Eureka Bandits. His family had made its money by outfoxing fellow minor timber barons in Humboldt County. A Eureka High School Logger bench-sitting third baseman in his playing days, Harvey had but one hit during his high school career. He talked about it endlessly. "It was a doozy," he'd say, making it sound like a home run. In reality it was an unintentional bunt misplayed by the catcher. Everyone knew it was an error except Logger scorekeeper Edith Klunk, Harvey's mom, who ruled otherwise.

Eudora Jones, the Arizona Gila Monsters owner, operated Jones Elixers, a cactus-based health juice operation headquartered in Mesa, Arizona. Eudora Jones spent much of her time fighting with state and federal labor authorities over the employment of Mexicans without proper papers. The labor battle was a constant draw, as Mexicans continued to crush cactus juice as well as their hands and arms while being denied workers' compensation benefits.

Lodestar owner, Barnaby Flum of Baker City, was a rowdy mechanic's apprentice who had married the spirited daughter of the owner of the Halfway Silver Mine. On their honeymoon she was "lost" at sea. After he was acquitted of all charges, Barnaby bought the local baseball team, installing his brother, Elmer, as General Manager. He then forgot about baseball, spending his time gambling instead. When brother Elmer wasn't involved with baseball, he authored anti-government pamphlets for the Baker City Liberty or Death Committee.

The Daily City Tender Loins were owned by Tiffany Macabre. Tiffany was a former entertainer with a hideously large Adam's apple, huge even for a man, which Tiffany once was. Her birth name was Ted Foyer, and before Ted became Tiffany, he was an ex-college baseball player and patent attorney. Tiffany made her name as a Bay Area celebrity, hosting a popular local TV show named, "Tiffany's Tips," with a focus on beauty and self-awareness. Tiffany's adam's apple was voted Best Celebrity Characteristic by the morning radio show "Richie and Dirty Phil," besting Dirty Phil's mole.

Bob Teetle, an ex-San Diego Padre reliever without career distinction, was the managing partner of the Las Vegas Showstoppers. His co-partners had names like Marty the Thumb and Thick Ricky. Teetle was fond of curling his lip and saying to people, "You look like Mickey Lolich and I hate Mickey Lolich." Also, he bit his nails and scratched himself inappropriately. At annual owners meetings, owners jockeyed to keep at least one seat between themselves and Teetle.

A stadium is the physical container of baseball. It is responsible for cradling the game, holding it in its soft arms, raising it above the civilian world. Ideally, a stadium must possess a charm equal to its game. Unfortunately, the only stadium in the Western Baseball Association to possess any historical charm was the Showstopper's boxlike venue built atop a failed silver mine. In Vegas, that's charm.

The Eureka field was once the high school baseball field, remodeled after an alumnus burned his alma mater to the ground.

The Tenderloins, similarly, used a former high school field, its left field fence a five story brick building. To be a home run the ball had to hit above a large horizontal white stripe that ran along the second floor. Memorably, it was an argument over whether or not a ball had hit above this white stripe that prompted the season-ending umpire walkout of 1982.

With less than three thousand seats available for baseball fans, Smelt Stadium had only been filled to capacity once. The first time was for Smelt legend Big Bat Boscowitz's final game. The other sellout was on the Fourth of July game against the Eureka Bandits in 1964. Earlier that day, a rumor had circulated around New Rotterdam that the Beatles were going to parachute into the stadium. When the British mop tops failed to descend from the sky, however, the betrayal had sparked the infamous 1964 New Rotterdam Beatle Riots.

Smelt Field, in its long march from bad design to eventual decay, had become little more than a garden of weeds with white lines drawn on it. Left field featured a small wild hedge growing near the fence. Outfielders routinely had to negotiate molehills. Right field was a dirt patch because it was the Garibaldis preferred dumping ground for rancid clam fry oil.

. . . .

"How's it goin', Little?"

"Feeling good, Grampie, feeling good."

Little was Jimmy "Little Bat" Boscowitz, Big Bat Boscowitz's uncoordinated grandson and current Smelt second-baseman. Grampie had a soft spot for his error-prone second sacker. After all, he and Little shared Smelt history. They were both princes of the realm. Grampie's father, a famed Smelt second baseman of the 1950s, and later, Smelt manager, was known in his playing days as the "Devilbridge Flyer." He was the Smelt record holder for stolen bases in a season.

"How's the ankle?" Grampie asked, having seen Little Bat twist it during warmups.

"Brand new," Little Bat said. "Good to go."

Little Bat was nimble in attitude, but nowhere else. Second basemen are prized when quick, with excellent hand-eye coordination, and able to range wide into their peripheries. Little Bat's game was more in the manner of being a tripping hazard.

Still, he was family. Smelt family.

"Hey, I almost forgot," Little Bat said, standing and thrusting out his hand. "Happy Birthday, you old coot."

Grampie, whose birthday was still a few months away, took Little Bat's hand and shook it.

"Thanks, Little. Thanks for remembering," he said.

From his experience, Grampie knew that truth was seldom good. In truth, Little Bat shouldn't have been on the roster at all, let alone in the starting lineup. But Grampie was only the manager of the team, not the owner of it. Gabriella Garibaldi thought Little Bat was cute, so that was that. Little Bat's position in the Smelt error machine was assured.

Grampie walked past the bench where his players sat in front of lockers, practicing spitting next to their shoes. He stopped at the exit. Without turning, he said, "Okay, boys, it's the Showstoppers. We hate them and they hate us. So let's not hit balls to Showstoppers, let's hit balls through 'em."

Then he turned to face the team. He waited until a few eyes were on him. "When you hit it, kill it," he said.

"Kill it," yelled Bang Bang, raising his fist in the air.

"Kill it," murmured a few of the rest, their voices hollow with the ennui that comes with knowing you can't play ball worth a whit.

. . . .

The Smelt had few staff employees, the most visible being Smelt mascot, Fishhook. Fishhook's primary function was was to dance with pretty girls atop the dugouts between innings while flinging cheap t-shirts into the crowd. The t-shirts were emblazoned with various Smeltisms. "Once A Smelt, Always A Smelt," "Smelt, Not Just A Fish," "Smelts Rule, Showstoppers Drool," "Have a Clam for Christmas."

Fishhook's costume was a pair of oversized denim overalls dyed silver, matched with a twenty-pound vacuum-formed plastic fish head with a wire fishhook in its mouth. Flecks of red paint dotted the mouth, intended to be seen as blood, but since the head hadn't been cleaned in twenty years, it looked like Fishhead ate rust. Inside, it reeked of clam. It is a Smelt irony is that Fishhook's head actually didn't look like a smelt. It looked like a dying salmon with acne. Never maintained or cleaned, it was pocked with beer can dents and stained by clam leavings. Fishhook's head appeared to have taken the blame after every Smelt loss. At least once a season, it got thrown up on by a kid from above who had overdosed on clams.

Fishhook was replaced each year only because no one ever asked if they could do it again. Therefore, each spring, a few unknowing New Rotterdam High Schoolers arrived at Smelt Field to interview with Gabriella Garibaldi for the position of Fishhook. This interview always began with Gabriella asking the same question: "Do you think you could dance without Fishhook's head falling off?" The head was top-heavy, difficult to maneuver; nonetheless, the job attracted weaklings. Never were there more than two applicants who, when trying on the head, could manage it. Ties went to the tallest, as Gabriella felt the physics involved in balancing Fishhooks head favored the tall. It didn't actually work out that way, but Gabriella was a clam monger, not a physicist. Essentially, all Fishhooks were the result of guesswork.

This season, Devilbridge High junior, Abel, was the only applicant who didn't drop the head when trying it on; therefore, he had no need to rely on his height of six feet, six inches for the job.

"You'll be our tallest Fishhook yet," said Gabriella as she pointed Abel toward Fishhook's head. "Treat it with care, young man. Former Fishhoooks everywhere are counting on you."

Abel was an instant hit as Fishhook. Smelt fans loved the tall, gawky teenager whose legs were still trying to figure themselves out while he pranced around trying not to fall down. They especially loved it when Abel danced perilously close to the edge of the dugout roof while gripping his head with both hands.

"Take one for the team," one helpful fan yelled.

"Make it a header," yelled another.

Baseball fans like to boo their own. Grampie described it this way: "Unlike the government, baseball belongs to the people. Have you seen people, lately? If you haven't, don't bother. It ain't pretty."

A first rule of baseball is the ball bounces where it wants to bounce, not where you expect it to bounce. The only reasonable way to overcome bad bounces is to employ superstition. Superstition is the mother's milk of ballplayers who suffer bad bounces. Ballplayers enjoy a variety of superstitious rituals. Some turn off the lights in a certain order when they leave home. Others don't change their socks or underwear. One Las Vegas Showstopper was said to drop a quarter into his favorite slot machine every morning at the Park-N-Ride next to the baseball stadium. Former Smelt Shel Otterdorf, during his brief journey through New Rotterdam, made it his habit before each home game to swipe a Snickers from the Walgreens on Washcon.

Abel's superstition was to visit Big Bat Boscowitz before each game.

. . . .

Near Smelt Field's entrance was a life-size cement sculpture of Big Bat Boscowitz. Boscowitz played for the Smelt for thirteen seasons. Even fans who'd never seen Big Bat play had heard of him because each September 27th was Big Bat Day, all concessions half price. Clam buckets, Bernie's beer, Smelt Cones, all half price. Big Bat's bobblehead was the most prized item at the Smelt Team Store, just besting the Fishhook key chain.

In Big Bat's final year, the last home game of the season was on September 27. The Smelt would finish third that year, tying their highest finish ever. On that day the Smelt were hosting the Showstoppers who were expected to win. The Showstoppers always won. They'd won the Western Baseball Association Finals twenty-three times in their history. The Smelt had won none.

The Showstoppers were up, 5-4 in the bottom of the ninth. It was the Smelt's last chance, the season finale. Dopey Troon was on first, having walked. Bitsy Spooner struck out, as did Dutch Clapp. Two out, a man on first, and to the plate for the last time in his baseball career strode Big Bat Boscowitz.

The crowd murmured support, having had little experience with hope in the bottom of the ninth.

"Hit one out, Big Bat," one yelled. Others yelled the same. It became an echoing chant. "Hit one out. Hit one out."

Smelt Mountain, Smelt Field's massive centerfield wall loomed 425 feet from home plate. At twenty feet high, only one person had ever hit a home run over it. That person was Big Bat. He'd done it in his rookie year. No one had come close since, except for Big Bat, who'd come close but no cigar a dozen times.

Showstopper closer, Xavier Cugat Brown, decided his first pitch to Big Bat would be a fast ball. Sadly for Cugat Brown, his fast ball wasn't fast enough. Big Bat swung, connected, and the ball arced into the New Rotterdam mist, heading toward Smelt Mountain. By the time the ball bounced off the topmost part of Smelt Mountain and back into play, Big Bat was already rounding second base. Unbelievably, the ball bounced the Smelt's way. When the Showstopper outfielder finally threw it to the cutoff man, and thence to the catcher at home plate, it was too late. Big Bat scored standing up. The Smelt had won! An inside-the-park home run. Lore, fable, the magic of baseball had come alive in New

Rotterdam. It remains the most famous play in the history of Smelt baseball.

Abel set the Fishhook head on the ground and stood quietly next to Big Bat's statue. He felt the legend's power flow through him, trusting it would make him more agile while dancing atop the dugout. He noticed a clam shred hanging off Big Bat's sculpted nose and flicked it away.

"Big Bat," he said, the grandeur of Smelt baseball halting his throat.

Abel picked up his fish head, put it on his head, settling it as Big Bat Boscowitz would have settled in the batter's box. Abel was ready for the game. New Rotterdam's annual Summer Begonia Festival had begun. Fishhook would dance the twist that day with at least one Begonia Princess, maybe two.

. . . .

Seattle Mariner announcer Dave Niehaus was Cletus Gum's idol as a boy. Young Cletus would mimic his idol all the time, practicing calling baseball games irrespective of where he was.

He could be in bed at night, in a Walmart aisle, at his school desk during class, or even in church.

"In the name of the Father, the Son, and the Holy Spirit," intoned Father Hasselquist at New Rotterdam's First Lutheran Church. Before the congregation could reply "Amen," the nave resounded with "Break out the rye bread and mustard, Grandma." Heads turned to see angelic Cletus Gum grinning like he'd just been given a free bucket of clams.

As suggested by Father Hasselquist, Mr. and Mrs. Gum made a deal with their son. They got him a voice recorder for Christmas if he promised to use it only in his room, and not too loud. Cletus agreed. Instantly he began recording himself mimicking sportscasters. Along with Niehaus, Cletus mimicked Joe Buck and Bob Costas. After convincing his parents to get the Major League Baseball channel, he reviewed old time great announcers like Harry Caray and Howard Cosell. Cletus Gum practiced his sports announcing voice, trying to find a sound that felt just right. But as much as he mimicked them, he couldn't get his mouth to make the sound he wanted. The voice he was looking for, his voice, eluded him.

"You can't just talk," Cletus told his parents. "You have to sound like someone. Someone great."

"Keep at it, honey," his mother said.

"And keep it down," added his father.

Cletus was passing the den one day. The TV was on and his mother was watching her favorite show, when he heard the voice. The voice he'd been looking for. It was a voice like no other. It had tenor and tone, resonance and clarity. It possessed sonic wavelength and amplitude.

"Who's that?" Cletus asked his mother. "That voice?"

"What, Lady Mary?"

"No, the man voice."

"Oh, you mean Lord Grantham? Yes, he does have a lovely voice, doesn't he?"

Mother Gum was a big supporter of public broadcasting. She thought public broadcasting was good for the brain. Her husband wasn't so sure.

"What's with Lord Grantham?" Mr. Gum wanted to know. "If I had a place that cool I sure wouldn't invite my relatives to come ruin it."

Cletus Gum, however, was after Grantham's voice, not his irritating in-laws. At last, he'd found a voice he wanted to emulate, a voice to explore. Lord Grantham's voice was perfect. It was a voice that could insult an umpire in one moment and be his best friend in the next. It was a voice without fear of retribution.

Cletus Gum practiced Lord Grantham's voice so diligently that he was forced to take throat lozenges and gargle with salt water. He practiced rapidly, reciting vowels and consonants front to back until they lost all distinction. Eventually, he felt ready. As a senior at New Rotterdam High, he applied to be the school's play-by-play radio announcer.

"Your voice has upper class demeanor," said a social climbing librarian who led the interview. "The job is yours."

It was a dream come true, and like all good dreams it kept expanding. After high school came New Rotterdam University where Cletus majored in media ecology and social justice. By his sophomore year at New Rotterdam University, radio listening fans could hear Lord Grantham calling Rottweiler baseball and football games on the college station, KROT.

After a couple of years on KROT, Cletus decided he needed a name that would better suit Lord Grantham, so he began referring to himself as Cletus Van Gum.

"It has more oomph," he told his mother who only said, "Don't tell your father."

Enchanted by fortune, Cletus Van Gum's college graduation coincided with an opening for the job of Smelt Field announcer. Applicants would face Gabriella Garibaldi. He was her first interview of three. The other candidates were a loudmouth who drank too much at the Bowsprit and a former Begonia Festival pitchman with a profound lisp. The only reason Gabriella agreed to give the lisper an interview was that she would be this year's honorary marshal during the Begonia Festival parade and decided it might not look good to snub him right away.

Cletus Van Gum was asked by Gabriella to introduce the starting lineup of the Smelt. "Just as you would in real life," Gabriella suggested. She offered him the lineup.

"That's okay," Cletus said, waving her off. "I already know it."

As he had planned, Gabriella looked impressed. "Go on," she said.

"Ladies and Gentleman," Cletus began, "Your attention please for the starting lineup for your maaagical Smelt."

"Excuse me, Mr. Van Gum, may I stop you? Do you know that you sound exactly like my very favorite television person."

"Really? Who's that?"

"Lord Grantham of Downton Abbey. It's my absolute all time top ten show."

"My mother's too," said Cletus.

"Well, I think I've heard all I need to hear. The job is yours if you want it."

"Maaagical!"

"Magical?"

"It's my signature call, Gabriella. I may call you Gabriella, yes?

Gabriella pushed back her chair and crossed her legs, affecting a girlish smile that didn't work. She was better with clams than girlish smiles.

Cletus Van Gum leaned forward in his chair, grabbed an imaginary microphone, and said, "Get ready, boys and girls of Smelt summer, it's your seventh inning stretch. Time to get a maaagical clam bucket. It's waiting for you at the Clam Shack concession stand. Better get 'em before they're all gone. You don't want to miss out on all the maaagic. Remember, it isn't a Smelt game without clams."

Gabriella stood and stuck out her chest first and hand second. "Lord Grantham, I believe you've just earned your first raise."

. . . .

As it was with every year, this would be another rebuilding year for the Smelt, a difficult challenge because the Smelt would field exactly the same team as played the previous year. No new talent, the same old non-talent. Still, by mid-season, the maaagical Smelt had already won five times, two more than the previous year at the same point in the season. But no one expected miracles, they expected another disaster. A Tribune sportswriter wrote, "The dreaded Las Vegas Showstoppers are in New Rotterdam for a three game series. Woe be to thee, Smelt."

The Showstoppers won the league the previous year with 54 wins against just 12 losses. The Smelt were dead last, 4-62, tying the club low set in 1952.

As it happened, the Smelt got slammed in the first game of the series, 12-1, three-hit by Ramon Kelp, the Showstopper's ace knuckleballer. In that game, in the bottom of the ninth with two outs, Elvis Prestige was on first due to having been hit in the ribs by an errant knuckleball. The next batter, Bang Bang, surprised everyone by hitting a not-so-sneaky fastball to the gap between center and right. It rolled to the base of Smelt Mountain. The Showstopper left fielder was unable to find the ball in the weeds. Several treasonous Smelt fans near the left field wall tried assisting the left fielder by yelling, "It's right there, dummy, by your foot." But it was too late. Elvis theatrically slid across home plate well before the ball reached the catcher's mitt.

"Safe," yelled the umpire. Elvis Prestige struck his fist into the air before doing a little quickstep dance that he'd been practicing. After the next batter struck out on three pitches, The fans cheered wildly.

"Yay. We only lost by 11."

. . . .

"Play Ball!" the umpire, a baritone, sang. "Play ball."

"The Showstoppers suck," fans crowed. "What Happens in Vegas Ought to Stay in Vegas."

It was game two of the series with the Showstoppers.

The Smelt hadn't beaten them, home or away, since Big Bat's last famous at bat. Still, Lord Grantham encouraged 613 paying fans, "Get your clam buckets ready, kids. Here comes some Maaagic."

Showstopper shortstop Miguel O'Toole, stepped to the plate. He faced Smelt rookie, Grant "Phenom" Lee.

When your nickname is "Phenom" you have nowhere to go but down. Even if a phenom becomes a competent pitcher whose ulnar collateral ligament stays intact, the name remains a curse. You might as well be featured on the cover of Sports Illustrated.

Grant "Phenom" Lee finished warming up. Each pitch had hit the dirt in front of home plate.

Miguel O'Toole dug in his cleats after spitting towards third base, catching most of it on his sleeve. Any veteran baseball man will tell you that you really don't hit your spitting stride until your mid-twenties. O'Toole was just nineteen.

"Phenom" Lee waited for Miguel O'Toole to twice wipe the spit from his sleeve and onto his pants. Finally, when he was ready, "Phenom" Lee got ready. The few fans who were paying attention got ready. "Phenom" Lee swiveled his body so that the number on his back was all that Miguel O'Toole could see. "Phenom" Lee uncoiled and let his first pitch fly. It was a laser, a fastball towards the heart of the catcher's mitt.

It never got to the mitt. Smack! The ball went over the right field wall instead. After rounding the bases, lithe Miguel O'Toole slapped high fives with his teammates in the Showstopper's dugout. The Smelt were down 1-0 and things went downhill from there.

"Phenom" Lee was lifted by Grampie in the third inning, the Smelt then down by eight. Manager Flatt had seen enough. "Now pitching for the Smelt," Lord Grantham nee Cletus Van Gum announced. "Randy 'The Maaagical' Owl."

"Whoo...Whoo," Randy Owl fans whistled.

The Showstoppers won, 17-0, as Miguel O'Toole went 4 for 4. Two games, two Smelt loses.

. . . .

When Smelt fans got excited, they made a sound known as Smelt Noise. It wasn't a word or a tone, just a noise. To make Smelt Noise, fans opened and closed their mouths like fish, emitting plosive pops of air. When one person did Smelt Noise, it sounded like someone with a nasal infection trying to get your attention.

Children got their introduction to Smelt Noise when standing in line at a Clam Shack. When it was their turn, the parent dangled a clam over an open-mouthed child. "What do you say?" the parent asked until the child made their initial attempt at Smelt Noise. It was a tribal event, as everyone else in line would give supportive murmurs of Smelt Noise.

"Good job, sweetie," the parent would say, dropping a clam into the little one's craw.

Sometimes a child continued doing Smelt Noise while at the same time they were chewing a clam with their mouth open. Parents frequently took this as an opportunity to socially groom their offspring.

"Don't make Smelt Noise with your mouth full."

. . . .

It was noon, game three against the Showstoppers. A light haze softened the bird blue sky. Grampie looked at his lineup. Only eleven Smelt were available to play. Three were out injured and three more missing. Right fielder Steelhead Mulroney's doctor, who sounded just like Mulroney, called to say Steelead had the the 24-hour flu again. It wasn't Mulroney's first time with the 24-hr flu.

Grampie once whined to Florabunda, "Steelhead got the bug again."

"Don't bug me," Florabunda laughed, her hair Cinnabar and Prune.

Third baseman Phil Samson phoned Grampie, then mimicked static noises, saying he was delayed in traffic. "Really bad. Worst I've ever seen."

"Do you want ketchup or mustard?" Grampie heard the Wompburger girl say, at which point Samson made more static noises and hung up.

Meanwhile, starting shortstop Manny Obstrepero was at his lawyer's office trying to figure out a plausible excuse for why he tried to use VISA cards that didn't belong to him.

"It's the Showstoppers, boys," Grampie said in his pre-game team talk. "We hate them and they hate us. So do what haters do best. Kick the shit out of someone."

"Yeah, let's kick some shit," shouted Bang Bang. Little gave his "Yeah" a half-hearted effort. The rest stared at their cleats.

Bang Bang, who led the league in errors by an outfielder the previous season, tripped on the steps coming up from the dugout, but didn't fall down. Instead he lunged forward, his arms flailing as he fought to retain his equilibrium.

"Kick ass, Bang Bang," shouted a man with pieces of clam flecked across his chin.

"Chitty-Chitty Bang Bang," a Begonia Princess cried out.

Once positioned in the field, Bang Bang spit on his shoe. Bang Bang was a veteran, but he still spit like a teenager. In the infield, Little Bat Boscowitz committed two warm-up fielding errors on one grounder. The ground ball came at him, hit a divot and bounced up, smacking him in the mouth. Little Bat scooped it up and hurriedly threw it over the first baseman's head, bouncing it off railing and into the stands where it barely missed a woman nursing a child.

"What a maaaagical day for baseball in New Rotterdam," enthused Lord Grantham. "Simply maaaagical."

Cute little Emily Clodhopper of the New Rotterdam restaurant family was escorted by the three Begonia Princesses to a microphone at home plate. Lord Grantham announced Emily would sing the National Anthem. In a firm voice, Emily said she was dedicating her performance to her grandfather who was at the Washon Senior Center. Requisite sounds of cute approval threatened to morph into Smelt Noise, but a sense of decorum and calm prevailed. Emily then launched into an ear splitting, off key rendition of the Star Spangled Banner, the words of which she only sort of knew. The Smelt Kings, two saxophone players down on their luck, tried to drown her out, but were outdone by the New Rotterdam Air Club's three Piper Cubs which buzzed the field just as Emily ended with, "I am so brave." She was escorted from the field by the Begonia Princesses. It resembled a perp walk.

....

Showstopper starter Alejandro Valdez had utterly bedazzled Smelt hitters through three innings, due mostly to his windup. Known as the "Pirouette," it was said to mesmerize batters into submission. Valdez, a native New Yorker, was a competitive salsa dancer in his youth. After one competition, a losing salsa competitor sliced a knife across Valdez's right cheek. The wound required twenty stitches and left his face looking like a torn map.

His nickname was "El Feo."

Valdez treated home plate with disdain. He hated batters. He moved his pitches around like a warlord positioning troops. A curling slider for lefties, high and in for righties. Tempo and control, each pitch a pas de deux. Sandwiched between two nasty heaters, a sinker would stalk the dirt. And when his victim was set up, a laser on the inside. Few timed him well, being too busy being intimidated. It is difficult to focus on swing technique when you think you've just shit your pants.

Alejandro Valdez had the physique of a young Clint Eastwood and the nasty look of a guy young Clint Eastwood couldn't kill.

Valdez stormed around the pitching mound like a malevolent despot, the dark altar from which he distributed damnation. He affected an unusually detestable mustache, a Fu Manchu with its tendrils dyed red. He said he wanted batters to think he was a vampire. Sometimes, between pitches, he took a step toward the batter and silently mouthed, "I want to eat your heart."

Valdez had faced nine Smelt already in the game, six with Ks on the scorecard, one opposite Little Bat's name.

"All I remember is hearing the thud," said Little Bat later, sitting in the dugout. He repeated it five times until someone said, "Yeah, Little, we get it. You can't hit."

. . . .

"Time for some of that old Smelt maaagic!" peppy Lord Grantham enthused.

When Grampie first heard Cletus Van Gum's voice he asked Florabunda, "How does a kid from New Rotterdam come out sounding like that?"

"He's a professional," she said.

It was the middle of the sixth inning, the Showstoppers up 7-0. Half the Smelt fans lined up for clams and beer, the other half angling to get a ride home early or looking for antacids.

Fishhook danced on the Smelt dugout with Begonia Princess Melodie who outweighed him by fifty pounds. They had started out doing the twist. Abel always did the twist because it didn't require Fishhook's head to move much. Princess Melodie, however, was a fan of swing, not twist. She grabbed Fishhook's hand swung him around a couple of times. She was just warming up. She locked arms with Fishhook and flung herself into the vastness of her joy. They flew off the edge of the dugout.

Abel landed first, Princess Melodie on top of him. Fishhook's head lay to the side, collateral damage. Abel, at first thinking his stomach had been pierced by his spine, struggled for air. Princess Melodie, unhurt but acutely embarrassed, found her feet and fled the field sobbing, trailed briefly by nascent Smelt Noise.

"Oh my God," one Begonia Princess said to the other. "Melodie can't swing."

The game stopped at once. Grampie and the umpires gathered around Abel. The players in the field clustered toward second base. The crowd murmured, a mix of gasps and groans. Grampie grabbed Abel by the belt, pumped him up and down a couple of times to get the breath back into him.

"Don't worry, son" Grampie said. "You just got the wind knocked out of you."

Abel gurgled his appreciation.

Then the bewitchment occurred.

It was one of those things time cannot explain.

It was a red flash. And it tore across Tier 2 past the Smelt front office, and down the corridor until it reached the announcer's booth. The red flash entered the booth.

It was Florabunda.

"Move over, Grantham," she said, grabbing the microphone from Cletus Van Gum.

Florabunda had been trying to catch Grampie's eye and ear earlier by the dugout. But with all the fuss on the field surrounding Fishhook's and Princess Melodie's mishap, she couldn't. She had to come up with a Plan B fast and this was it.

"Grampie. Grampie. It's me. I'm up here," she shouted into the microphone. Everyone in Smelt field, fan and player, including Abel and the Begonia Princesses, turned to look to where the voice was coming from.

"Grampie. Guess what?" Florabunda shouted into the microphone.

Grampie did not move. The crowd stilled.

"Guess what? Grampie. Guess what?" Florabunda repeated.

Grampie stared at the booth. Was that really her? Was that crimson bouffant really Florabunda's?

"Guess what?" Florabunda repeated. "Guess what?"

"For crying out loud," shouted the crowd. "What?"

"I won the Lotto, Grampie. I won the big one."

The crowd gasped. Grampie's spine tingled. The Begonia Princesses hugged each other. Bang Bang and Little, by second base, fist bumped.

"I won the Lotto, Grampie. I won the Lotto." Florabunda waved the Lotto ticket in the air. "Stay there, I'm coming down. Don't move. I'll be right there."

Abel, now standing, indicated he was okay, but Smelt trainer, Dr. Felgaard, wanted to be sure. Dr. Felgaard wagged two fingers in front of Abel's eyes and asked, "How many thumbs am I holding up, son?"

"Two," Abel said.

"Let's give him a few more minutes," Dr. Felgaard said.

By the time Dr. Felgaard felt Fishhook sufficiently recovered, Florabunda had arrived field side. She stood near the dugout amid a crush of fans. Cletus Van Gum, who felt the maaagic and wasn't about to miss the moment, was next to her with a portable microphone.

"Grampie, over here," Florabunda shouted. She waved the Lotto ticket at him. "It's the big one. Five million smackeroos."

Grampie yelled back. "Are you sure?"

A fan wearing glasses had rested his chin on Florabunda's shoulder. She showed the fan both her ticket and the winning number printout. The man took his time examining them. Everyone was on edge. The Smelt Kings did a short riff.

At last, the inspecting fan with the glasses lifted up his head and shouted, "She ain't lying, folks. It's the big one. Red won the big one."

A new kind of Smelt Noise erupted, a sound no one had heard before. Grampie later described it as "the sound of redemption." He told Florabunda he saw a halo around her head, "like you were golden."

Grampie turned and signaled to the home plate umpire, indicating he wanted to talk. They stepped away from the others. Grampie talked, the umpire listened. The umpire talked, Grampie listened. When done talking, Grampie turned and walked over to Florabunda who had been lifted onto the field by some gentlemen Smelt fans.

Grampie embraced Florabunda and Florabunda embraced Grampie.

And Cletus Van Gum, having climbed over the fence after Florabunda, used his absolute best Lord Grantham voice when speaking into his microphone. "Remember this day on your deathbeds, Smelt fans. You were here. You were at Smelt Field on its most maaagical, maaagical day ever."

Grampie stood next to Florabunda who stood next to Abel. Grampie turned to Abel. "Son, I don't think you're cut out to be a fish," he said. "Try managing instead." He took off his ball cap and placed it on Abel's head.

"I can't believe it," Lord Grantham proclaimed. "Now managing for the Smelt, Fishhook. How bloody maaagical is that?"

The crowd went bananas. "Fishhook. Fishhook," they chanted. "Grampie Flatt. Grampie Flatt. Maaagical. Maaagical." As Grampie and Florabunda exited Smelt Field, every Smelt player was standing and clapping, several Showstoppers among them, some raising their right fists in solidarity, all hoping Grampie would remember them at Christmas.

"Ladies and gentlemen, there he goes," Lord Grantham said in a particularly elegant tone. "The most maaagical Smelt of all time. Grampie Flatt. And let's not forget his red-headed good luck charm. Goodbye, Grampie Flatt. Goodbye good luck charm." Then he turned to face the crowd. "Come on Smelt fans, let's send them off in style." He began singing "Take me Out to the Ballgame."

"Just think," Florabunda said on their way to the car, squeezing his shoulder. "No Smelt has had a standing O since Big Bat."

Grampie, with his arm around Florabunda, said to the heavens, "Beat that baseball."

. . . .

In the eighth inning of a game three weeks after Grampie left the team, Little Bat Boscowitz hit his first career home run. The week after that he hit two more. All three were maaagical. And a couple of weeks after that he hit two more homers off a Eureka Bandit in a single game. Little Bat ended up hitting .373 for the remainder of the season and was voted a Western Baseball Association all-star. And it wasn't only his bat that got hot, his errors halved. And it was obvious to even the greenest Smelt fan that his base running was much less boneheaded.

The Tribune's sportswriter wrote, "Smelt fans, rest easy. Little Bat finally fits his granddad's shoes."

During the home stretch of that baseball season, Grampie and Florabunda were sitting on extra-comfy folding chairs at the RV camp grounds at Escalante National Monument in Utah. They sat beside their new Coachmen Leprechaun, sipping raspberry-infused tequila from Waterford crystal highball glasses, on which were engraved HIS and HERS.

Grampie told Florabunda she was right. He didn't only like Utah, he loved it. He loved its space, its wide boundaries. "No nothing but being free," he said, looking off into the wide blue sky.

"Told you I'd win the Lotto," Florabunda said.

"Not only that," said Grampie. "You hit it out of the park."

Florabunda put her hands up to her face, coquettishly. "I bet you say that to all the Smelt girls."

She wore a new turquoise bracelet she'd bought for her upcoming photo-shoot for "RV Beautiful." She'd met the publisher at the RV Convention in Salt Lake City.

Grampie looked at his cell phone, checking the news. They sat quietly in that vastness known as Utah.

After awhile, Grampie said, "I'll be. The Smelt won the league. They're champions. The Smelt are champions."

Florabunda's hair was red peach with pinkish tips. She wore oversized sunglasses and looked dazzling. Two gardeners had already run into each other after seeing her.

"Maaagical, honey" Florabunda said, pretending to be Lord Grantham. "Simply maaagical."